"Is there anything else I should know about you?"

Cade's tone was light and teasing, but his eyes darkened as his gaze moved over her.

Feeling like a doe caught in the headlights, Callie shook her head.

"Come now," he said, taking a step closer. "You must have some other secrets hidden away." He lifted one brow. "I know you like taffy and chocolate. And being kissed."

She licked lips gone suddenly dry as he moved toward her. "Cade…"

"Talk to me, Red. Tell me about you. I want to know everything." He brushed his lips over hers. "Your likes." He kissed the tip of her nose. "Your dislikes." His hands folded over her shoulders, drawing her up against him.

"I…" She swallowed hard, unable to speak, unable to think when he was holding her so close, when he was looking down at her like that, his eyes filled with fire and desire.…

Dear Reader,

If you can't beat the summer heat then join it! Come warm your heart with the latest from Silhouette Romance.

In *Her Second-Chance Man* (SR #1726) Cara Colter enchants us again with the tale of a former ugly duckling who gets a second chance with the man of her dreams—if only she can convince him to soften his hardened heart. Don't miss this delightful story of love and miracles!

Meet *Cinderella's Sweet-Talking Marine* (SR #1727) in the newest book in Cathie Linz's MEN OF HONOR miniseries. This sexy soldier promised to take care of his friend's sister, and he plans to do just that, even if it means *marrying* the single mom. A hero's devotion to his country—and his woman—has never been sweeter!

Talk about a fantasy come to life! Rescued by the handsomest Native American rancher this heroine has ever seen definitely makes up for taking a wrong turn somewhere in Montana. Find out if her love will be enough to turn this bachelor into a husband in *Callie's Cowboy* (SR #1728) by Madeline Baker.

Lilian Darcy brings us the latest SOULMATES title with *The Boss's Baby Surprise* (SR #1729). Dreams of her handsome boss are not that strange for this dedicated executive assistant. But seeing the confirmed bachelor with a *baby?* She doesn't believe it…until her dreams begin to come true!

We hope you enjoy the tender stories in this month's lineup!

Mavis C. Allen
Associate Senior Editor

Please address questions and book requests to:
Silhouette Reader Service
U.S.: 3010 Walden Ave., P.O. Box 1325, Buffalo, NY 14269
Canadian: P.O. Box 609, Fort Erie, Ont. L2A 5X3

Callie's Cowboy

MADELINE BAKER

SILHOUETTE *Romance*®

Published by Silhouette Books

America's Publisher of Contemporary Romance

My thanks to the National Registry of Historic Places
for allowing me to quote from the historical plaques
on the buildings and historical sites.

Thanks, also, to…Judy Boles, Shelley Dietrick, Baird Todd,
Karla and Karlee for their help in supplying me with information
on Montana and Virginia City.

And especially to Ty Perry for answering my many questions.

And to Kim Ivora for catching my mistakes.

Thanks, all. I couldn't have done it without you.

SILHOUETTE BOOKS

ISBN 0-373-19728-4

CALLIE'S COWBOY

Copyright © 2004 by Madeline Baker

This edition published by arrangement with Harlequin Books S.A.

Visit Silhouette Books at www.eHarlequin.com

Printed in U.S.A.

Books by Madeline Baker

Silhouette Romance

Dude Ranch Bride #1642
West Texas Bride #1697
Callie's Cowboy #1728

MADELINE BAKER

has written over twenty historical novels, half a dozen short stories under her own name and over seventeen paranormal novels under the name Amanda Ashley as well as Madeline Baker. Born and raised in California, she admits balancing her love for historical romance and vampires isn't easy—but she wouldn't like to choose between them. The award-winning author has now found another outlet for her writing—with Silhouette Romance! Readers can send a SASE to P.O. Box 1703, Whittier, CA 90609-1703 or visit her at her Web site http://madelinebaker.net.

Montana Man

I met a man who rescued me
A cowboy brave and wild and free
A hero as untamed as the sod
Where his Lakota ancestors had trod

He opened to me a world so new
He taught me all that I could do
If I would turn from all my fears
Put away my doubts and foolish tears

He made me believe if I'd but try
That with the eagles I could fly
He brought me joy, he brought me laughter
He promised me happy-ever-after

He offered me love like I never knew
Made all my hopes and dreams come true
And in return I took his hand and
Gave my heart to my Montana man
                    —Callie Walker

Chapter One

Callie Walker knew she was staring, but she just couldn't help it. The man was, without doubt, the most gorgeous creature she had ever seen. Not just cute. Not just handsome. But heart-stoppingly, drop-dead gorgeous. Being a romance writer, Callie had seen more than her share of good-looking guys. Tall, blond and tan, or tall, dark and mysterious, they graced the covers of her books, wrapped around equally gorgeous females. Hunky male models and wannabe models turned up at writers' conventions and conferences where they were ogled by romance readers, both young and old. There were contests where the models and wannabe models blatantly strutted their stuff before legions of adoring female fans.

But this man…oh, lordy, he was the most delicious hunk of masculinity she had ever seen. He had smooth copper-colored skin and well-defined cheekbones that hinted at Native American blood. Straight black hair fell to the middle of his back. His cutoff T-shirt and tight-fitting jeans revealed the kind of broad shoulders, muscular arms, long legs and taut tush that made women swoon.

In short, he was cover-model material from the top of his head to the run-down heels of his black cowboy boots.

He turned away from the cash register and his gaze locked with hers. His eyes were an earthy shade of brown framed by thick black lashes.

Callie felt a blush climb into her cheeks at being caught staring. Apparently he was used to it. Touching one finger to the brim of the black cowboy hat pushed back on his head, he gave her a knowing wink and a roguish grin and walked out of the coffee shop.

With a sigh, Callie glanced down at what was left of her dinner, now grown cold, and pushed the plate away and went to pay her check.

If she hurried, she could make another hundred miles before dark.

Cade Kills Thunder couldn't help grinning as he left the coffee shop and walked across the street to where he'd parked his rig. He was used to women gawking at him. Usually, he just ignored them, but there had been something about that one. What, he couldn't say. She had a sprinkling of freckles across her nose and cheeks, and she wore her long red hair tied back in a ponytail. To top it off, she was short and a little chunky, not his type at all. He liked tall willowy females with blond hair and blue eyes, women who were happy to spend a day or a night in his company, women he could love and leave without a second thought. He couldn't swear to it, of course, but he was willing to bet that Ponytail Red was the "till death do you part" type.

Definitely not for him. He was the "love 'em and leave 'em" type. Had he been a sailor, he would have had a woman or three in every port. Driving a big rig cross-country gave him pretty much the same opportunity as going to sea, only better.

He was still grinning when he climbed into the back of the rig to get some shut-eye.

Chapter Two

Callie opened her eyes wide and then rolled her shoulders in an effort to keep awake. She needed to pull off the road and soon, before she fell asleep at the wheel. She had planned to stop at the next motel she saw, only she never saw one.

Frowning, she glanced at the wrinkled Montana road map spread out on the passenger seat beside her. She had obviously taken a wrong turn somewhere along the way; unfortunately, reading a map had never been her strong suit and she had no idea where or when she'd gone wrong.

Darn it! She wouldn't be in this predicament if she weren't so afraid to fly. She knew it was a totally irrational fear. She had no reason to be afraid of flying. She had never had a close call while in the air, had never come close to crashing. In fact, she had never even been on a plane. But she knew, in some deep, dark corner of her mind, that the minute she boarded an airplane, it was doomed to experience engine trouble or lose a wing, plummet to earth and explode in flames. Her best friend kept telling her that when it was her time to go, she'd go, but Callie was determined that, when her time came, it wouldn't be on a plane!

She scrubbed her hand over her face. She was so darn tired. If she could only close her eyes for a moment. She glanced at the surrounding countryside. There were no street-lights, no friendly motels with brightly colored neon signs blinking Vacancy, just acres of moonlit fields and the seemingly endless black ribbon of road ahead of her.

Maybe she should just pull over for a few minutes and take a quick nap.

She dismissed the thought immediately. In her line of work, having a vivid imagination was a plus, but right now it was a definite hindrance. She could all too easily envision some maniac attacking her while she catnapped, or being whisked into an alien spaceship like the one on *The X-Files*, or kidnapped by some rabid fan à la Stephen King.

Yawning again, she turned up the radio and switched on the air conditioner, hoping the noise and the cold would keep her awake until she found a cozy motel.

Cade stretched the kinks out of his back and shoulders. Another hour or so, and he'd be home. As much as he hated to admit it, he needed this vacation. Lately, he had put in too many miles on too many highways. He was more than ready for a little R & R, ready to head for the local watering hole and swap tales with Norton and Housley or play a little nine ball with Dockstader. He was ready to drink a little and dance a little and, if he got lucky, score a little with that new waitress, Molly What's-her-name, over at the Broken Spur Saloon. The home place was in need of a little tender loving care, too. He was going to have to repair that hole in the barn roof before winter set in. The house needed a fresh coat of paint. The hinges on the corral gate had to be replaced. And it had been a while since he'd checked the water holes.

He shook his head ruefully. When he got home, his great-grandfather would likely give him hell for being gone for so long.

Thinking of the old man brought a smile to Cade's face. Jacob Red Crow was eighty-two years old and all Indian. He still adhered to the Old Ways. In the summer, he slept in the ancient hide teepee pitched in the backyard. Jacob would have slept out there in the winter, too, if Cade hadn't insisted he sleep inside. Sometimes Cade wondered why he worried about the old man so much. Jacob was in better health than most men who were ten years younger, and while his eyesight might be growing a little dim and his hearing questionable, Jacob's mind and his tongue were still sharp. Even though Jacob Red Crow could be as stubborn as a mule and as bossy as a hen with one chick, he was one of the few people Cade genuinely admired and respected.

Cade blinked, rubbed his eyes and blinked again. Was he seeing things? No, that was definitely a car nosed into the ditch up ahead. He whistled under his breath. It was a classic 1955 Thunderbird, turquoise-blue with a white top. Sweet, he thought, mighty sweet. And mighty lucky. Another couple of feet down the road, and the car would have been wrapped around a tree.

Out of habit, he checked the road behind him before pulling the rig to a stop in front of the T-Bird.

Grabbing his flashlight, he opened the door and swung out of the cab.

Shining his light into the car, he saw a woman slumped over the steering wheel. Dead or unconscious, he couldn't tell. He tried the door, but it was locked. Using the end of his flashlight, he rapped lightly on the window, once, twice.

The woman inside stirred and he rapped on the window again.

With a start, she raised her head and looked out at him, her eyes wide with fright.

"You okay?" he called.

She blinked at him.

"Hey, Red, you okay in there? Open the door."

She stared at him through wide eyes that were the soft gray of a dove's wing. It didn't take a rocket scientist to know what she was thinking. He was a stranger and she was on a deserted road, alone in a car late at night.

"You need help." He touched his forehead. "You're bleeding."

She lifted a hand to her head, frowning when her fingertips came away stained with blood.

"Open up, Red." He rapped the end of his flashlight on the window again. "If I wanted to hurt you, all I'd have to do is break the window."

She considered that for a moment, and popped the lock.

Opening the door, Cade dropped down on his haunches, putting him at eye level with the woman. He studied her in the glow of the flashlight. "Do you hurt anywhere else?"

"No."

"What happened?"

"I guess I fell asleep. I woke up just in time to avoid hitting that tree."

"And ended up in a ditch." The front end of the T-Bird was in pretty bad shape and one tire was flat. Reaching into his back pocket, he pulled out a kerchief and handed it to her.

"Thank you." She pressed the cloth to her forehead. "I need to call the Auto Club."

"No phones around here, sweetheart."

"I have a cell phone." Leaning over, she picked her handbag up off the floor and rummaged around inside, finally producing a phone. "Shoot! The battery's dead."

"Don't worry about it. Come on, I'll take you to my place. You can call from there, or I can send Sam out to pick up your car."

"Your place?" She shook her head. "I don't think so." She frowned at him a moment. "It's you." Her eyes widened with recognition. "You were at the coffee shop."

"That's right." He held out his hand. "Come on, you can't stay here."

She glanced from his face to his hand and back again. "You're not some kind of serial killer, are you?"

He laughed. "Would I tell you if I was?"

"No," she said, a blush pinking her cheeks. "I don't suppose so."

"You got a name?"

"Callie. Callie Walker."

"I'm Cade Kills Thunder," he said. "I can show you my driver's license, if you like. Credit cards, Boy Scout salute, whatever it'll take to ease your mind."

"I guess I really have no choice but to trust you." She took the kerchief from her head, frowning when she saw the blood.

"Right. Come on." Taking her by the hand, he helped her out of the car. "Anything you need?"

"My things are in the trunk."

With a nod, he pulled the key from the ignition and opened the trunk. "You want *all* this stuff?"

"Yes, please."

Muttering under his breath, Cade switched off the flashlight and shoved it into his back pocket, then pulled a large suitcase out of the trunk, along with a smaller case, a garment bag and a laptop computer.

He carried it all to his rig and stowed it in the sleeper compartment, then went back for the woman.

He found her standing in front of her car, looking as if she were about to cry. "I can't just leave it here," she wailed softly.

"Trust me, sweetheart, it'll be fine." He turned off the lights, rolled up the window and locked the door. "The only people who use this road are people who live hereabouts."

She shook her head. "Do you know what I paid for this?"

"I can't imagine," he said gruffly.

She let out a little shriek when he swung her into his arms and carried her to his rig.

Callie caught a quick glimpse of a big white truck, with a red, white and blue eagle painted on the door, before he lifted her into the cab. In her books, he would have been a tall, dark hero wearing a white hat and riding up to rescue the heroine on a flashy white stallion. She couldn't help smiling a little at the image, or the similarity. This hero was tall, dark and handsome, but instead of one horse, he drove a big rig that probably had a couple hundred horses under the hood. The only discrepancy was his hat. It was black.

Grunting softly, Cade shut the door, then walked around to the other side of the rig and swung up behind the wheel. "Put your seat belt on."

Feeling a trifle uneasy in the presence of a strange man, even if he did seem to be rescuing her, Callie settled into the big leather seat and did as she was told. "I've never been in one of these before. Is this your truck?"

He blew out a sigh. "In the first place, it's not a truck— it's a tractor. And, yes, it's mine, so sit back and enjoy the ride." Checking his outside mirrors, he put the engine in gear and pulled out onto the road.

"How far is it to your place?"

"About thirty-five miles."

"Thirty-five miles! Isn't there a motel or something closer?"

"'Fraid not. How'd you get on this road anyway?"

"I don't know. I guess I missed a turn."

"Where are you headed?"

"Virginia City."

"You missed a turn all right. A couple of them. It's about fifty miles back the other way."

She blushed again. "I never could read a map. So, where am I now?"

"Dillon's the nearest town. So, are you here on vacation?"

"Not exactly. I'm doing research for a book."

He glanced at her. "You're a writer?"

"Uh-huh."

"So, what do you write?"

"Books."

He lifted one brow in wry amusement. "Is that right? I never met a genuine author before. What kind of books do you write?"

"Romance novels."

He looked at her a moment, and then grinned. "Lots of purple prose and heaving breasts, that kind of thing?"

"I don't write purple prose," she replied indignantly.

Cade chuckled, aware that he'd hit a nerve. He had never read a romance novel, of course, but his sister Gail loved them. Loved them? That had to be the understatement of the century. She devoured them, sometimes reading two or three a week. Next time she called, he'd have to ask her if she had ever read any of Red's novels.

"So," he asked, "how many books have you written?"

"Nine."

"No kidding? Good money in it?"

"Good enough. How long have you been a truck, er, tractor driver?"

"About twelve years."

"Good money in it?"

She was quick, he thought with a grin. "Not bad. Depends on the mileage and what you're hauling."

"What do you haul?"

He shrugged. "You name it, I've probably hauled it. Produce, cattle, car parts."

"Twelve years," she mused. "I guess you must like driving. The freedom of the open road and all that."

He didn't deny it. He liked the feel and the growl of the

engine, liked being his own boss, too, and if he pushed the rules a little, well, that was his business and nobody else's.

She glanced around the cab. It was set up pretty much like a car, though the console was bigger. It had high bucket seats with a gearshift in the middle, a radio and a CD player, one of which was playing Native American flute music, turned low.

She frowned when she noticed the heavy gray curtain that ran behind the seats, closing off the cab from the rest of the rig. "What's back there?"

"Sleeper compartment."

"You've got a bed back there?"

"Yep. And a TV with a built-in VCR. And a refrigerator."

Looking impressed and a little surprised, she murmured, "All the comforts of home."

"More or less."

"Do you sleep back there very often?"

"Often enough." He didn't spend much time watching the TV but some nights, after a long day behind the wheel, he couldn't get the image of the road out of his mind. On those nights, when he couldn't get that yellow line out of his head, he shoved a tape into the VCR. It distracted him enough so that, in a matter of minutes, he could sleep.

"Seems like a lonely life to me," she remarked.

"I reckon that's why I like it. How's your head feelin'?"

"Kind of sore."

"You should probably see a doctor."

"Oh, I don't think so."

"You might have a concussion."

"I don't like doctors."

He shrugged. "Suit yourself."

She fell silent and he turned his attention to the road. This stretch, narrow and winding and lined with tall trees, was also a deer crossing.

When the road straightened out again, he glanced over at his passenger. He wasn't surprised to find that she had fallen asleep, her head pillowed on her arm.

She was going to be trouble, he thought with a rueful shake of his head. Big trouble.

Chapter Three

Cade parked his rig alongside the barn, killed the engine and then spent a few moments studying his sleeping passenger. There was a dark bruise on her left temple, a bit of dried blood matted in her hair. He had a sudden urge to stroke her cheek and see if her skin was as soft as it looked, to run his hand through her fiery red hair and see if it would burn his fingers.

A romance writer. He shook his head. He had met women from all walks of life, married, single and in-between, but he'd never met a romance writer. He supposed everyone she met asked how she researched her love scenes. Looking at her now, he couldn't help pondering that same question.

Muttering an oath, he swung out of the cab, walked around to the passenger side and opened the door.

"Hey." He shook her shoulder lightly. "We're here."

Her eyelids fluttered open and she stared at him blankly. "Here?"

"My place. Come on." Slipping an arm around her waist, he lifted her from the cab. He was about to set her on her feet, but found that he rather liked holding her in his arms. Settling her more comfortably against him, he carried her up to the house.

"I can walk, you know," she murmured, but she seemed perfectly content to let him carry her.

The front door was unlocked. He carried her inside and up the stairs to the room his sister used when she came to visit.

"I think you'll be comfortable here." He sat her down on the bed, then turned on the light. "The bathroom's at the end of the hall." He plowed his fingers through his hair. "Make yourself at home. I'll go down and get your things."

"Thank you."

With a nod, he left the room.

Callie glanced around. It was a large room furnished with antique oak furniture. The walls were papered with a soft green-and-rose stripe. Frilly white curtains covered two large windows; a painting of wild horses running through a stream hung on one wall. There were several framed photographs on the dresser. She recognized Cade in one of them. He was standing beside a pretty girl with long black braids and a sunny smile.

She looked up as he entered the room.

"Here you go." He dropped her suitcase and garment bag on the floor at the foot of the bed, deposited her laptop on the desk in the corner.

"Thank you."

"Can I get you anything?"

"Some aspirin?"

With a nod, he left the room, returning a few minutes later with a bottle and a paper cup, filled with water, which he handed to her. "Anything else?"

"I don't think so. Oh, is it all right if I use the phone to call the Auto Club?"

"No need. I'll send Sam after your car first thing in the morning."

"Who's Sam?"

"He helps out around here from time to time. He can tow your car into town."

She thanked him politely yet again, wishing as she did so that she could come up with some better dialogue.

"No problem. My room's the last one on the left at the end of the hall if you need me."

She nodded. He was a big man, broad in the shoulders and narrow in the hips, and he carried himself with an air of self-confidence that she found daunting. She wasn't used to big men. Actually, she wasn't used to men at all. Writing was a lonely profession. The few close friends she had were other writers, all female.

"Good night, Red."

"Good night."

Whistling softy, Cade closed the door behind him and went downstairs. In the kitchen, he plugged in the coffeepot and then poked around in the fridge, looking for something to eat. There wasn't much of a choice—a couple of wrinkled green apples, a six-pack of cola, mustard, blackberry jelly, mayonnaise and dill pickles.

With a shake of his head, Cade grabbed the jelly and a soda. He was surprised the old man didn't starve to death. There was bread and peanut butter in the cupboard and after making himself a sandwich, he took his soda and went out on the front porch.

Dropping into the old rocker, he propped his feet up on the rail and blew out a deep breath. It was good to be home.

"Hey, Kola." Reaching down, he scratched the old hound dog behind the ears. "How you doin', fella? Been out chasing rabbits?"

The dog whined, then stretched out at Cade's feet.

Cade blew out a sigh. Knowing the woman was inside made the house feel different somehow. Made him feel different somehow.

He had never brought a woman here before. He had dated

more than his share of pretty ladies. Hell, he had even been engaged for a week or two a few years back, but he had never brought any of his dates home. Of course, Red wasn't a date and he hadn't really brought her home, at least not in the usual sense. He lifted the can and took a long swallow. He couldn't very well have left her out on the road in the middle of the night.

He grunted softly. A romance writer. He had always pictured them as middle-aged women who wrote love stories because they weren't getting any at home. But this woman…he shook his head. She wasn't beautiful and she wasn't his type, but there was something about her.

"Don't even go there," he muttered. For all he knew, she could be married with a couple of kids. He dismissed that notion out of hand. If she was married, he was pretty sure she would have been calling home.

Well, married or not, she wasn't his problem. He'd ask Sam to haul her car into Dillon tomorrow morning and later in the day, he would take the woman into town and drop her off. That would be the end of it.

Callie woke slowly. Stretching, she glanced at her surroundings and then jackknifed into a sitting position. Where was she? Frowning, she reached up to brush a lock of hair from her face, winced as her fingers hit a rather large bump on the side of her head.

She remembered then. She had fallen asleep at the wheel and when she woke up, there was a man standing outside her car. Oh, yes, she remembered him! That tall, dark drink of water she had seen at the coffee shop. The same one she had been fantasizing about before she fell asleep.

This was his house.

Slipping out of bed, she tiptoed across the floor and pressed her ear to the door. Was he up yet? Did she dare take a shower?

Hearing nothing, she pulled her robe on over her nightgown, grabbed a change of clothes and hurried down the hallway. The bathroom door was invitingly ajar. She slipped inside and shut it behind her.

Cade looked up from the stove as his great-grandfather came in the back door. "Mornin', *Tunkashila*."

"*Hau.* Is that bacon I smell?"

"That it is. I went to the store early this morning. It was that or starve."

Jacob Red Crow shrugged, then glanced upward as the shower came on. Frowning, he looked back at his great-grandson, a question in his eyes.

"We have company," Cade explained, turning the bacon.

"Who?"

"A woman. I…"

"A woman!" Jacob smiled broadly. "It is about time."

"It's not like that, *Tunkashila*. She was in an accident last night. I found her in a ditch on the side of the road." Cade scrambled a dozen eggs in a bowl and poured them into a pan. "Sam took her car into town this morning."

"She is the one."

A shiver slid down Cade's spine. "What do you mean, the one?"

"She has red hair, yes? And gray eyes."

"You saw her?"

Jacob nodded solemnly.

"When?"

"Last night, in my dreams."

Cade knew better than to disregard Jacob's visions but, in this case, the man was way off base. Cade had no intention of settling down any time in the near future and when he did, it would be with a tall willowy blonde, not a short redhead with a smattering of freckles on her nose.

"You need a wife," Jacob said. "It is not good for a warrior to live alone."

"I thought you didn't approve of our people marrying outsiders."

Jacob shrugged. "This *wasicun winyan* is different."

"Is that right?"

"Han."

Opening the fridge, the old man pulled out a can of dog food and went outside to feed Kola.

With a shake of his head, Cade stirred the eggs, added some salt and pepper and a bit of hot sauce, turned the heat down under the bacon and put some bread in the toaster. Luisa hadn't been good enough for Cade's father, but Jacob had decided that this romance writer, a woman Jacob hadn't even met yet, was the right woman for Cade?

He was still muttering to himself when his guest entered the kitchen, her ponytail swinging behind her.

She smiled tentatively. "Good morning."

"Mornin'," Cade replied. He jerked his chin toward the table. "Sit down. Breakfast is ready."

"Is there anything I can do to help?"

He shook his head. "I'm not much of a cook, so don't expect too much."

"He needs a woman in his life."

Cade scowled as the old man entered the kitchen. "Callie, this is my great-grandfather, Jacob Red Crow. Jacob, this is Callie Walker."

A broad smile lit up the old man's face as he offered Callie his hand.

"I'm pleased to meet you, Mr. Red Crow."

"Thank you." His grip was firm as they shook hands. "It's nice to meet you, too, Miss Walker. But you must call me Jacob."

Still grinning, the old man dropped into the chair across from hers and poured himself a cup of coffee from the pot sitting in the middle of the table. He gestured at the cup in front of her. "Can I fill that for you?"

"Yes, please."

She couldn't help staring at the old man. His skin was the color of old saddle leather, lined and creased by time and the elements. His black braids were streaked with gray. He wore a pair of faded jeans, a calico shirt, a black leather vest and moccasins. In spite of his age, he looked lean and fit.

Cade put a plate heaped with bacon, eggs and hash browns in front of her. He handed one to his great-grandfather, and then sat down.

Jacob Red Crow covered his potatoes and eggs with ketchup; Cade doused his with salsa, then offered Callie the bottle.

"No, thank you."

With a nod, he turned back to his breakfast.

Jacob swallowed a forkful of eggs, then smiled at Cade. *"Lila waste."*

Cade grunted. "You think anything is good as long as you don't have to cook it."

Jacob looked at Callie. "Can you cook?"

"Of course." She pushed the bacon to the side of her plate, then took a bite of her eggs. Delicious.

A faint smile twitched the old man's lips as he glanced at his great-grandson, then lit into his breakfast again.

Callie glanced around the kitchen as she ate. It was a large sunny room. The cupboards were dark oak. The refrigerator was an old side-by-side. The stove looked new. There were no pictures or knickknacks of any kind. The only decoration was a hoop of some sort with feathers hanging from it. The table and chairs were also oak.

"Callie, here, is a writer," Cade remarked after a while.

Jacob looked at her expectantly. "Like Tony Hillerman?"

"Well, not exactly. He writes mysteries." She felt her cheeks grow warm. "I write romance novels."

Jacob nodded. "Those are good, too."

Cade stared at his great-grandfather. "How would you know?"

"I've read some."

Callie hid a smile behind her hand. This was obviously news to Cade.

"What name do you write under?" the old man asked.

"My own. Callie Walker."

The old man slapped his hand against the tabletop. "I thought your name sounded familiar."

Rising, he hurried from the room and returned moments later with one of her books in his hand. He dropped it on the table beside Cade's plate with a look that clearly said, "Told you."

Cade looked at the couple on the cover and scowled. There was a white man, dressed up like an Indian, holding a pretty blond female who was falling out of a dress that no pioneer woman would ever have owned, much less worn in public.

"I'd be happy to autograph it for you before I go," Callie said, smiling at the old man.

"I'd like that." Jacob looked at Cade and grinned. "How about that? I'll have an autographed copy."

"Yeah, great. So," Cade said, glancing over at Callie, "what made you become a writer?"

She shrugged. "It was the only job I could think of that I could do at home in my nightgown."

She knew it had been the wrong thing to say the moment the words had left her mouth. She could think of another job, often called the oldest profession in the world, that would have allowed her to work in her nightgown.

Judging from the look on Cade's face, he had thought of it, too.

"Plus I have a good imagination," she added quickly. "And I enjoy it."

Cade grunted softly. "Why don't they put real Indians on your covers?"

"I don't know. I really don't have anything to say about that. It's decided by my editor and the art department."

Jacob Red Crow nudged Cade. "Maybe you should take up modeling."

The old man was kidding, of course.

And Cade laughed out loud.

But Callie didn't laugh. She looked at Cade, then at her book cover and had a brilliant idea.

Chapter Four

Cade pushed his plate aside and stretched. When he started to clear the table, Callie rose to help him.

Jacob pushed away from the table and took the plates from her hands. "Grandson, why don't you show Miss Walker around the ranch? I'll do the dishes."

Cade looked at her skeptically, one brow arched. "Do you want to take a look around the place?"

"I'd love to, if you don't mind." She smiled at Jacob. "And please, call me Callie."

Jacob beamed at her. "Go along with you now. I'll look after things here."

Cade seemed less than enthusiastic about playing tour guide, but Callie was eager to explore the ranch. There was a cattle ranch in the setting of her next book.

Cade led the way outside. Callie paused on the porch, invigorated by the clear Montana air, overwhelmed by the vast blue vault of the sky and the mountains in the distance. The view was breathtaking.

Hurrying down the stairs, she followed Cade toward several large corrals. Two of the pens held horses, one held a cute little spotted calf and the fourth held a full-grown buffalo.

Callie stopped and peered through the rails. She had seen buffalo in movies, of course, but never a live one and never close up.

She jerked backward as the animal shambled toward her. She could see that it was limping. Lordy, but it was big, and the closer it got, the bigger it got.

She glanced at Cade as he moved up beside her. "Do you raise buffalo?"

He chuckled. "No, Clyde's a pet. We've had him since he was a calf. Jacob found him out on the prairie a couple of years ago."

"What's the matter with his leg?"

"It was broken when Jacob found him. Never did heal right."

"Poor thing."

"Yeah. I wanted to make buffalo burgers out of him, but the old man wouldn't hear of it."

Callie whirled on him, her eyes flashing. "Buffalo burgers! How could you? He's beautiful…"

Laughing, Cade held up his hands in surrender. "Hey, I was just kidding."

She glared at him a minute, then grinned sheepishly. "Sorry. I just hate to see animals abused."

"Yeah, me, too. Come on."

She followed him toward the big red barn located across from the buffalo corral. Several horses whinnied and stretched their necks over their stall doors as Cade entered the building.

"You like to ride?" he asked.

"I don't know. I've never been on a horse."

"City girl?"

She nodded. The horse in the nearest stall poked its nose

over the door, snuffling softly. It was a pretty animal, with a glossy black coat and a tiny white patch on its forehead.

"Hey, Ohanzee." Cade scratched the horse between the ears, then reached into his pocket and withdrew an apple. He offered it to the horse, who ate it with a great deal of noise and gusto. Foamy apple juice dribbled from the corners of its mouth.

"What does Ohanzee mean?"

"It means shadow in Lakota."

"It suits him."

"Her."

"Oh. Sorry, girl."

Cade grinned, charmed by the woman in spite of himself.

He moved on down the aisle, stopping to talk to all of the horses, giving each of them a treat of some kind—an apple, a lump of sugar, a carrot, a peanut-butter-and-jelly sandwich.

Callie shook her head. "Peanut butter? And jelly?"

"She loves it," Cade said.

Still shaking her head, Callie followed Cade out of the barn.

"How big is your ranch?" she asked.

"About a hundred and sixty acres. We raise some beef cattle and run a few head of horses."

Callie came to a halt when they rounded a corner of the house and she saw the teepee. Though she was no expert, she thought it looked like the real thing. She glanced at Cade, one brow raised.

He nodded. "It belongs to Jacob. He likes to sleep out here in the summer."

"Not in the winter? I thought Indian lodges were warm." At least, that's what her research books said.

"They are, but he's old and…" Cade shrugged. "I worry about him out here, alone."

She smiled, touched by his concern for his great-grandfather. "Do you think we could…?"

"Could what? Oh, you want to look inside."

"If you don't think he'd mind."

"Sure, come on."

Cade lifted the lodge flap and motioned for Callie to go inside. It was far larger on the inside than it looked from the outside. In spite of all the research she had done for her books, she'd never had the opportunity to explore an authentic Lakota lodge. There was a firepit in the middle of the floor, with an opening directly overhead to allow the smoke to escape. A pile of furs was laid out near the back of the teepee. Jacob's bed, she supposed. There was a Thunderbird shield on a tripod, a few pots and pans stacked near the doorway. A couple of hide bundles and small pouches hung from the lodge poles.

She stood there a moment, absorbing the feel of the place. It smelled faintly of smoke and earth and something she thought might be sage.

"Sweetgrass," Cade said when asked. "The Lakota use it in some of their ceremonies and for healing, that sort of thing."

Callie nodded. She had learned as much from the research she'd done.

As Cade showed her around the ranch, she wished she had brought her camera with her. She would have loved to take some pictures of the buffalo.

She slid a sideways glance at Cade. And of the man.

He really was amazing looking, with his coppery skin, long black hair and intense brown eyes. And those shoulders, almost as wide as a barn door. He'd look marvelous on the cover of her next book.

"Well," she said as they returned to the house, "I really should be going. If it isn't too much trouble, could you give me a ride to town?"

He nodded, though he was suddenly reluctant to see her go. "Maybe we should call the garage first, see if your car's ready."

"No need. If it's not ready, I can always get a hotel. I've imposed on you enough already."

Jacob was waiting for them on the porch when they returned to the house.

"I'm afraid I've got bad news for you, Callie," he said. "Walter over at the garage called. He said the front end of your car needs some extensive bodywork and a new radiator. Walter said he'll have to call around and see if he can find one in Butte or Helena."

"I guess radiators for a '55 Thunderbird aren't a stock item," she said glumly. "Is there anyplace where I can rent a car? I wanted to do some research in Virginia City before the convention starts."

"What convention is that?" Jacob asked.

"There's a writers' convention in Jackson Hole."

"No problem. Cade, here, will be glad to drive you to Virginia City. He can give you a first-class tour of the town, and then he can drive you on over to Jackson Hole. Isn't that right, grandson?"

Callie glanced at Cade, wondering if he was as surprised by the old man's words as she was. She felt a little thrill of excitement. If Cade would drive her to Jackson, she would be one step closer to turning her brilliant idea into reality. Still, it was a lot to ask of a virtual stranger.

"Thank you, but I really don't think I can ask him to do that."

"You aren't asking him, I am," Jacob said, brushing her objection aside. "Besides, it'll do the boy good. He's supposed to be on vacation, but if I don't get him away from this place, he'll spend all his time working. He needs to go have some fun for a change."

Callie was pretty sure that Cade didn't appreciate his great-grandfather arranging his vacation for him. One quick look at his face confirmed her suspicions. He didn't look happy about being drafted into the position of chauffeur and tour guide, and the last thing she wanted was to be in the company of a man who wanted to be anywhere except with her.

"It's too much to ask," she said, "really. If one of you can just drive me in to town, I'll rent a car."

"We won't hear of that, will we?" Jacob said, giving Cade a little poke in the ribs with his elbow.

A muscle twitched in Cade's jaw before he said, "No. I'll go get my things together. We can leave whenever you're ready."

Jacob Red Crow winked at Callie, then beamed at his great-grandson.

An hour later, Callie climbed into Cade's pickup truck. Jacob sat in the rocking chair on the front porch, slowly rocking back and forth, a hound dog sprawled at his feet. The old man waved as Cade slid behind the wheel and turned the key in the ignition.

As Cade put the truck in gear and pulled out of the yard, Callie couldn't help thinking that the old man looked mighty pleased with himself.

Cade didn't seem inclined to talk as he drove so Callie stared out the window, going over what she knew about the Big Hole Valley as she watched the scenery pass by.

As soon as she had decided to set her book in a town in Montana, she had called the Beaverhead Chamber of Commerce, and they had sent her a ton of literature on Dillon, Virginia City and the surrounding area. She had learned that early trappers had used the word "hole" to describe mountain valleys, and that the Big Hole Valley was known by several other names, including the Big Hole Basin and the Big Hole Prairie. Hay was the valley's only crop, which wasn't surprising. If she remembered correctly, each cow in a herd consumed something like two tons of hay over the winter. Haystacks weighed as much as twenty tons and stood about thirty feet tall, giving the valley another of its names, the Valley of Ten Thousand Haystacks.

Cade stopped in Dillon to fill the truck with gas, and then they were on the road again.

"Dillon seems like a nice town," she remarked as they left the gas station behind. "I'll have to come back and take a look around some time."

"It's been here a while. Lewis and Clark came through here back in the early 1800s. A lot of the old houses have been preserved. Descendants of John Bishop still live in his house. And be sure to take a look at the Wikidal House. The tower itself is worth the trip."

Nodding, Callie made mental notes for future reference. She loved doing research for her books. Of course, she couldn't go to all the places she wrote about, so she did a lot of research online and out of books, but there was nothing like seeing the place you were writing about firsthand.

"Any others?" she asked.

"The Orr Mansion's worth taking a look at. It was built in the early 1860s. Until recently, the mansion was still in the family's hands. Then there's the B.F. White house. White and some businessmen purchased a ranch and it became the townsite of Dillon. White was the president of the State Bank, the town's first mayor, and the state's last territorial governor. He passed away in 1923."

"Has your family always lived here?"

"For the last sixty years or so," he replied. "Jacob brought his wife here when they were first married. She passed away a couple of years ago and I came to stay with Jacob."

"What about your grandparents?"

"They're both gone."

"I'm sorry."

Cade nodded. "He died of pneumonia about five years back. She passed away a few months later."

"Do your parents live around here, too?"

"They live over on the next ranch. It used to be all one

property, but when my dad got married, Jacob split the land and gave half to my folks."

"That was nice of him."

"Yeah, especially since he didn't approve of my mother."

"Why not? What's wrong with her?"

He slid a glance in her direction. "She's not Indian."

"Oh, I see," Callie said, though she didn't see at all.

"My mother's Italian," Cade explained. "Jacob thinks she's some kind of witch."

"A witch? My goodness, why?"

"She sees the future sometimes, and she gets these feelings when something bad is going to happen to someone in the family. That kind of thing." Cade chuckled. "It's odd that he feels that way, since he's something of a psychic himself."

"Really?"

Cade nodded, but saw no need to tell her that Jacob had predicted that she "was the one."

"So, is your great-grandfather still upset because your mother isn't Indian?"

"No, he got over it a year or so ago." Cade laughed out loud at the astonished expression on her face. "Hey, I'm kidding. I'm pretty sure he forgave her when I was born."

"You must see your parents a lot if they live, well, next door."

"Usually, but they're in Italy right now. It's their anniversary this month and my mother wanted to go home and visit her mother and her brother and sisters."

"I've always wanted to go to Italy," Callie remarked. "Maybe I'll set a book there one of these days. It would give me a good excuse to visit. Be a good tax write-off, too. Whereabouts in Italy does your grandmother live?"

"Palermo."

"How long have your folks been married?"

"Forty years."

"That's a long time." Especially in this day and age, she thought, looking out the window again. It was hard to imagine anyone staying married for forty years. But she would! Several of her girlfriends had already been married more than once. Her own parents had separated last year, making her more determined than ever that when she married, not only would it be for better or worse, it would be forever.

She slid a glance at Cade and asked the question uppermost in her mind. "Why aren't you married?"

"Me?" He stared at her as if she had just suggested he take off all his clothes and jump into a pile of cactus. "No way, Red. I'm not a marrying man. Between ranching and trucking and looking after Jacob, I don't have time for a wife." He looked thoughtful for a moment and then added, "To tell you the truth, I've played the field so long, I don't think I could settle down and be faithful to just one woman."

"Why buy the cow…" she muttered.

"What?"

"Just something my grandmother used to say. You know, why would a man buy the cow if he can get the milk for free?"

Cade chuckled. "Exactly."

"Do you get a lot of free milk?" she blurted, then clapped her hand over her mouth, appalled that she had asked a man who was practically a stranger such an intimate question.

He laughed out loud, amused by her question and her obvious embarrassment at having spoken it aloud. "I've known a lot of up-front girls in my time, Red, but you take the cake."

"I'm sorry." She looked out the window to hide her blush.

"Let's just say I'm not real thirsty and leave it at that, shall we?"

She nodded, still refusing to meet his gaze.

She was grateful when they reached Virginia City.

Until she had started doing research for her book, she had assumed that the only Virginia City was in Nevada.

Cade found a parking place and they walked down Wallace Street. She fell in love with the town immediately. She didn't know what it was about old towns that she found so fascinating, but love them she did. There were countless ghost towns and old mining towns throughout the West and she intended to visit all of them, given the time and opportunity.

Of those she had already toured, Silverton, Colorado, was one of her favorites, even though it wasn't really a ghost town. She had been to Ouray and Montrose. Jerome, Arizona, was another town she had enjoyed visiting. She had been to Durango, as well. While not a ghost town, it still had a lot of history. She loved Virginia City, Nevada, and Bodie, up in Northern California.

Virginia City, Montana, was equally wonderful. The buildings were made of wood, old and weathered. Some of the stores were still doing business; some were for display only, with waist-high, fencelike barriers to keep people from walking off with the goods on display.

They passed the Smith and Boyd Livery Stable and the Bale of Hay Saloon, Sauerbier's Blacksmith Shop and the S.R. Buford Store, which was the town's first brick building and a regional supplier of groceries until 1881, when the railroad reached Butte. She peeked inside, fascinated by the display, certain that many of the fixtures and products were original.

She came to an abrupt halt to read another sign.

Built in 1899, one can see that this imposing structure was the pride, not only of Virginia City, but also of Montana—being, according to history the largest mercantile store in the state at that time. Hardware, hay, grain, salt, and groceries were available, AND WHISKEY BY THE BARREL! Original site of the Wells Fargo Co. from which the well known Wells Fargo Coffee Shop justly derives its name.
The Virginia Trading Co.

She was aware of Cade standing behind her, his arms crossed over his chest like a cigar store Indian.

Moving on, she stopped at the McClurg and Ptorney Mercantile-Wells Fargo Display. The building had quite a history. The space had held a restaurant, a United States Post Office and a bowling alley, among other things, before Wells Fargo moved in.

Many of the buildings also had plaques declaring that the property contributed to the Virginia City Historical District and that they were listed in the National Register of Historic Places by the United States Department of the Interior, in cooperation with the Montana Historical Society.

She had to stop and read each one, of course, and learned a lot about the town along the way.

Stopping in front of the Dance and Stuart Store, she read,

"James Stuart and his brother Granville set up the first sluice boxes in the northern Rockies in 1852. Delaware native, Walter B. Dance came to Gold Creek in 1862. James Stuart and Dance opened their mercantile in November 1863. One of Virginia City's most complete and respected shops, Dance and Stuart also briefly housed the post office. Clubfoot George Lane, reputed member of the infamous Plummer gang, lived at the store and was arrested there by the Vigilantes in 1864. A year later, the Montana Historical Society was founded in the building. The original Dance and Stuart was demolished circa 1925 and Charles Bovey built this replica of vintage logs in 1950."

From a pamphlet, she learned that Virginia City was located high in the Rocky Mountains in a bowl along Alder Gulch. Gold was first discovered in the Gulch in 1863. Within a year, the population of the town grew to more than ten thousand people. The city was the territorial capital from 1865 to 1875.

They walked to the end of the buildings, then turned and walked down the other side of the street.

She stopped at the Hangman's Building and read that vigilantes hanged five road agents in the building before it was completed.

They passed the Elling Bank and the Masonic Temple, which, at thirty thousand dollars, had been the most expensive building in the territory. The original furniture was still in use and had been shipped to Virginia City by steamboat and ox team.

The Montana Post and Print Shop stood on the corner. It had housed the territory's first newspaper, the *Montana Post*.

Cade trailed behind Callie, amused by her enthusiasm for a bunch of old buildings. She oohed and aahed as she peered in windows and made copious notes in a little notebook. He had never realized that romance writers actually did any research for their books. Maybe there was more between the covers than he thought.

She scurried off to the next building and he couldn't help admiring the sway of her hips, or the way the sunlight brought out gold highlights in her ponytail. He had never cared much for red hair, but he had to admit Callie's was mighty pretty.

She went into Rank's Drug Store and bought several books on Montana history, as well as a T-shirt and a couple of postcards.

Her next stop was Cousin's Candy Store, where she bought about five pounds of taffy. He couldn't blame her. He didn't have much of a sweet tooth, but Cousin's candy was the best he'd ever tasted. Thinking about Jacob, he bought the old man some of the hard candy he favored.

Callie smiled at him as they waited in line at the cash register. "Look, isn't that cute?"

He turned in the direction she pointed, and frowned. What was so cute about an odd-shaped green glass jar that wasn't more than a couple of inches high and, as far as he could tell, wasn't good for much of anything? She put her candy on the counter and went to pluck the jar from the shelf.

"I'm getting hungry," Cade remarked as they left the store. "How about you?"

"I could eat something."

They went to the Bale of Hay Saloon. Callie grimaced when Cade ordered a buffalo burger and fries

"Hey, it isn't Clyde," he said with a wry grin, "so stop looking at me like that."

"I'm sorry, I just think it's awful to kill animals for food."

"C'mon, Red, it's what they were put here for. My people have been eating buffalo for hundreds of years."

He shook his head when she ordered a lettuce-and-tomato sandwich and a double chocolate malt. "Don't tell me you're a vegetarian?"

Her chin came up defiantly. "Do you have a problem with that?"

He lifted his hands in a gesture of surrender. "No, ma'am." Leaning back in his chair, he decided it might be wise to change the subject. "So, just how much research do you do for one of your books?"

"Depends on the book. If it's a historical, I have to do quite a bit. I have to be sure to check names and dates because if I get anything wrong, you can bet one of my readers will catch it and let me know about it. Contemporaries would be easier, I guess."

He grunted softly. "Why do you write about Indians?"

"Because I like them."

He lifted one brow. "Really? How many do you know?"

"None," she admitted ruefully, and then, reconsidering, she grinned. "That's not true any more. I know you and your grandfather."

He leaned forward a little. "Think you know me, do you?"

His words were light and teasing, totally at odds with the smoky expression in his dark eyes.

Callie blinked at him as a jolt of sexual awareness sizzled between them. "I didn't mean…that is…"

She felt a rush of heat in her cheeks. Darn! She wasn't good at flirting, could never think of those cute little comebacks that seemed to come so readily to most of the women she knew.

Cade cursed inwardly. What the devil had made him say such a thing? He leaned back in his chair again as the waitress arrived with their order. He couldn't help noticing the becoming blush in Callie's cheeks, couldn't believe she was embarrassed by what he had said. It had been a harmless remark, perhaps a little suggestive, but not the least bit off-color.

Feeling suddenly self-conscious, Callie lowered her gaze, concentrating on her lettuce-and-tomato sandwich as though it might jump off her plate and run away if she didn't watch it every moment.

When they finished lunch, Cade trailed along behind her as they walked through the town again. This time, she stopped to take pictures of all the buildings and all of the signs. She took photos of Wallace Street from both ends, then stopped in front of Kiskadden's Stone Block.

As many times as Cade had been to the town, he'd never stopped to read any of the historical data. But he did so now, peering over Callie's shoulder while she scribbled some notes.

Virginia City's first stone building, constructed during the summer of 1863, originally housed three stores on the ground floor and a meeting hall upstairs. Popular legend has long designated this as the meeting place of the Vigilantes, who prosecuted and hung two dozen outlaw road agents in Virginia City between 1863 and 1864. Grocer William Kiskadden, the original occupant, married the former Mrs. Jack Slade after Slade was hung by the Vigilantes. Blacksmith George Thexton remodeled the building as a livery in the early

1870s, removing one of the two original center doors to enlarge the entrance and reusing it on the hay loft above.

"It certainly didn't pay to run afoul of the Vigilantes, did it?" she muttered.

Their last stop was the Virginia City Museum, which contained a variety of antiques, china, old documents and other memorabilia, including, of all things, the mummified clubfoot of George Lane.

"Good old George," Callie remarked. "Wasn't he one of the bad guys that the Vigilantes hung?"

"I think so," Cade agreed.

Callie nodded. Old George's cane and straight razor were also on exhibit. She wasn't the least bit surprised to find that there were picture postcards of his foot for sale.

Finding a mummified foot should have prepared her for what she saw next, but it didn't. Located on a shelf among an assortment of china and other collectible items was, of all things, the body of a petrified cat. According to a helpful note in front of the cat, the animal had apparently crawled under a house that was being built sometime in 1868 and had been found there years later by a Mrs. Emslie, no doubt a day that Mrs. Emslie never forgot.

Callie was still shaking her head over finding a dead cat on display next to the period china when they turned onto Idaho Street. Callie paused in front of the Bennett House County Inn, charmed by the quaint beauty of the house.

"I'd love to stay there someday," she murmured as they made their way back to Cade's truck. She glanced down the street, her expression wistful. "Gosh, I hate to leave."

"There's still Boot Hill," Cade said, hoping to cheer her up a little.

She brightened immediately. "Can we go there?"

"Sure."

A short drive took them to the cemetery that overlooked the town.

Callie was equally enthused at the sight of a handful of graves. She stopped in front of the Boot Hill sign.

Cade read over her shoulder, while she read out loud.

"This was Virginia City's first Cemetery. There were many markers here but only those of the road agents and Daltons remain. The road agents' graves, which give the cemetery its name, Boot Hill, were first marked by the city in 1907.

"William and Clara Dalton were no relation to the notorious gang nor connected with the road agents.

"They came to Bannack in 1862 with Captain James L. Fisk's first wagon train. They moved to Virginia City in 1863. William and Clara died of natural causes in January 1864, leaving four children. The grave was marked by a granddaughter many years later."

Making a small sound in her throat, she moved on.

Cade read a couple of the markers. Boone Helm, Hanged January 14th, 1864. George Lane "Clubfoot George" Hanged January 14th, 1864.

"Poor George," Callie remarked. "He's buried up here and his foot's in the museum."

"I doubt if he misses it," Cade remarked drily.

Callie grinned at him. "Well, come the resurrection, I suppose he'll get it back."

He had to laugh at that, and she laughed with him. Then his gaze met hers, and suddenly they weren't laughing any more.

Chapter Five

Cade couldn't say what, but there was something about Callie, something about the way she looked at him through those wide blue-gray eyes, as if he were Tonto and the Lone Ranger all rolled into one. Something about the light in her eyes and her unbridled enthusiasm for a beat-up old town. Something about the sweetness of her smile and the sound of her laughter that made his heart ache, but in a good way.

He moved slowly toward her, giving her plenty of time to back away.

But she didn't back away. Just stood there, her eyes growing wider as he drew closer. She swallowed hard as he slid one arm around her waist.

He gazed down at her, waiting to see if she would lean into him or slap him for his impudence.

She did neither, only continued to stare up at him, her eyes growing darker.

He whispered her name and then, unable to resist the need rising within him, he lowered his head and kissed her.

Cade enjoyed kissing, and not only because it usually led to other equally pleasant diversions. He had kissed a lot of women in his time—young ones who were still innocent and curious, older ones who had years of experience. But, after all was said and done, a kiss was still just a kiss. He hadn't expected Callie Walker's kiss to be any different from all the rest, but it was. Every other kiss he had ever known had been a warm-up for the big time, like playing baseball in the minors and then graduating to the major league. But Red's kiss out-classed them all. If there had been a World Series championship for kissing, she would have won it, hands down.

Standing on her tiptoes, she sighed and pressed herself against him, and his body came painfully, achingly alive. He slid his other arm around her and drew her up against him, hard and tight.

She was suffocating. Between the pounding of her heart and the force of his kiss, Callie couldn't breathe, couldn't think. Didn't want to think. She had been kissed a few times in her life, but never, ever, like this! Cade kissed her with a single-minded intensity that drove every other thought from her mind. His lips were warm and firm, his chest a wall of muscle, flattening her breasts as he drew her even closer. Heat exploded in the pit of her stomach and spread to every nerve and cell in her body until she was certain she was going to melt like ice cream left too long in the sun, until nothing remained but a puddle of warm liquid.

Feeling a little disoriented, she stared up at him when he let her go.

It was only then that she realized several other tourists had arrived. But instead of taking in the sights of Boot Hill, the three men, three women and five kids were staring at her and Cade.

Callie had written hundreds of thousands of words of dialogue in the course of her career but at that moment, she couldn't think of a single, solitary thing to say.

Cade muttered an oath, then took her by the hand and dragged her across the dusty ground to where the truck was parked. Wordlessly, he opened the door for her, then went around to the driver's side, slid behind the wheel and jammed the key into the ignition. The truck roared to life.

Callie turned away from the window, her head lowered, as they drove past the tourists who were still gawking at them.

"You'd think they'd never seen two people kissing before," Cade said, his voice a low growl of irritation.

"Well, they probably haven't," Callie mumbled, still mortified. "At least, not in the middle of Boot Hill."

Damn, if she didn't have him laughing again.

It served to ease the tension between them, at least a little.

"So," Cade said as they left the cemetery behind, "do you want to drive into Jackson tonight, or go back to the ranch and get a fresh start in the morning?"

"Whatever you want to do is fine with me," she replied, not quite meeting his gaze. "You're the one doing the driving."

"You're the one with a schedule to keep. It's about a five-hour drive to Jackson, which will put us there about…" Cade glanced at his watch. "Eleven."

"I guess we should leave tonight," Callie decided. "I'm supposed to attend a literacy book signing tomorrow at two-thirty."

With a nod, Cade pulled onto the road and headed for the highway.

He glanced at his passenger from time to time. Along about eight o'clock, she slumped sideways in the seat, her head pillowed on her hand, which rested against the window.

It somehow felt good to have her there.

About nine-thirty, he pulled off the highway to fill up the truck and get a cup of coffee. She didn't stir, so he left her sleeping in the truck while he went inside. He bought himself a large cup of coffee and another for Callie, just in case she woke up somewhere down the road.

Ten minutes later, he pulled onto the highway again.

Callie sighed and tried to find her way back to the wonderful dream she'd been having. Cade had been about to kiss her and she desperately wanted to feel his mouth on hers. But someone was shaking her shoulder and calling her name.

She came awake with a start when she realized that the man shaking her shoulder was the very man she had been dreaming about. Sitting up, she ran a hand over her hair.

"We're here," Cade said, pulling up in front of the Snow King Resort. "I hope you've got a reservation."

"What? Oh, of course I do. Oh! Where are you going to stay?"

"I'm sure I can find a room somewhere."

She hesitated for the space of two heartbeats, then said, "There's an extra bed in my room. You can have it, if you want. I mean, it's already paid for, and it's the least I can do when you've been so nice, driving me here and all, and…"

Her voice trailed off. She was suddenly glad that it was dark inside the truck. She was sure her cheeks were flaming. She had only meant to offer him a place to sleep. What if he had mistaken her offer of a bed for something else? Something more?

"Thanks," Cade said.

He cut the engine and got out of the truck.

She watched him walk around to her side and open the door. When he offered her his hand, she took it and he helped her out of the truck. She couldn't remember any other man having done that for her.

It was quiet inside the lobby. Callie glanced around, liking the feel of the place. It was done in rich earth tones. The carpet was a sort of dark-green-and-rose print, there were lots of plants, and trees in huge pots scattered around the floor.

The fireplace was impressive. Made of rock, it was four stories high.

There were vases of flowers on the reception desk; a pair of television screens were mounted on the wall to the right of the desk, one above the other, showing the hotel's events. She could see the pool through the glass, also to the right of the desk.

Callie checked in and the man at the desk told her where to park.

"I'll go out and get our bags," Cade said, "and meet you in the room."

"All right."

Callie checked her room number, relieved to see that it was on the ground floor. She wasn't crazy about heights.

Opening the door, she flipped on the light switch, and smiled. It was a lovely room, with a view of the Grand Tetons and the surrounding mountains. The carpet was mauve and white duvets covered the beds, which had lodgepole headboards. There were six pillows and a bolster on each bed. Tiffany-style lamps sat on the nightstands, which she thought were made of pine. An armoire held a twenty-seven-inch TV, complete with remote and cable service. There were several framed photographs on the walls.

She walked across the floor to the desk, admiring the lamp with its stenciled oiled paper shade. There was a chair at the desk, another in the corner near the windows.

She peeked into the bathroom. It had everything, from a full-length mirror and vanity lights to a tiled floor, as well as a hair dryer, lotion and shampoo.

There was a coffeemaker, of course. What hotel room would be complete without one?

She turned as Cade entered the room carrying their luggage. Her garment bag was draped over his shoulder.

"Where do you want me to put your stuff?"

"On the bed, I guess." She took the garment bag from him and hung it in the closet.

"Which bed do you want?" he asked.

"The one near the window."

With a nod, he dropped her suitcase and overnight bag at the foot of the bed. "Nice room."

Callie nodded. Heat rose in her cheeks as she glanced at the two queen-sized beds separated by nothing more than a nightstand and a few feet of floor space. She had never shared a room with a man before, especially one who was virtually a stranger.

Opening her suitcase, she pulled out her nightgown and robe, picked up her overnight case and fled to the bathroom.

Cade blew out a sigh. Suddenly, agreeing to share a room didn't seem like such a good idea. Every time he looked at Red, he remembered the kiss they had shared on Boot Hill. And every time he remembered that kiss, he wanted a whole heck of a lot more than just a kiss.

Damn!

He heard the shower come on and clenched his fists as he imagined her standing under the spray. With a shake of his head, he went to the window and stared out into the darkness. He was behaving like some randy teenager for crying out loud.

Needing something to distract him, he pulled his clothes out of his duffel bag, hung them in the closet and stuffed his underwear in a drawer.

That done, he tugged off his boots, scooped up the remote for the TV, then sat on the bed, his back against a mountain of pillows, clicking through the channels until he found an old John Wayne western.

The Duke had just laid into one of the bad guys when the bathroom door opened and Callie stepped into the room. She had brushed out her hair and it spilled over her shoulders in a riot of beautiful thick red waves that tempted his touch. He curled his hands into fists to keep from going to her, from running his fingers through her hair to see if it was as soft as it looked. She looked younger, prettier, with her hair unbound.

He could see her bare feet and the hem of a white nightgown peeking from beneath her robe.

She smiled tentatively. "I left you some hot water, if you want to take a shower."

"Thanks," he muttered. Rising, he tossed the remote on her bed and headed for the bathroom. Closing the door, he undressed and stepped into the shower. Hot water was the last thing he needed, he thought irritably. Teeth clenched, he turned the cold water on full blast.

Callie stared at the bathroom door, trying not to imagine Cade Kills Thunder standing in the shower, water running over his wide shoulders and broad chest and down his flat stomach ridged with muscle...

She jerked her thoughts from that direction and sat down on the bed. What was the matter with her? She had never been one to go gaga over good-looking guys. After all, she saw lots of them in her line of work. Every writers' conference, every convention, seemed to have its share of cover models strolling around. She had met most of them, been to lunch with a couple of them, been propositioned by one of them. But Cade Kills Thunder was different. He wasn't a celebrity. He wasn't looking for fame and fortune. He was real. And that was why she wanted him, but only for the cover of her next book, she told herself.

"You just keep telling yourself that," she murmured as the water went off in the shower.

Tossing the remote onto his bed, she took off her robe, slipped between the sheets and pulled the covers up over her head, feigning sleep.

But she couldn't help peeking at him through lowered lashes as he emerged from the bathroom a few minutes later. He was wearing his jeans and nothing else. His long black hair was still damp.

She wondered if he was going to sleep in his jeans, or...she closed her eyes again, refusing to go there.

He switched off the TV.

He locked the door and turned off the lights.

She heard the sound of cloth sliding over his legs as he took off his jeans, the faint creak of the bed as he slid under the covers.

Usually, it took her only minutes to fall asleep, but not tonight. Every time she closed her eyes, she saw Cade Kills Thunder silhouetted in the bathroom doorway, his long black hair as sleek as ebony, his skin a warm coppery color, his stomach ridged with muscle, and his arms…

She remembered all too clearly how those arms had felt wrapped around her when they had kissed. And now he was sleeping only a few feet away, wearing nothing more than a pair of shorts. Or maybe nothing at all!

Chapter Six

Callie opened her eyes, looked at her watch and groaned softly. Eleven a.m. She never slept this late, she thought, throwing off the covers. And then, remembering that she wasn't alone in the room, she pulled the blankets up to her chin and glanced at the other bed.

It was empty.

With a sigh of relief, she sat up, clutching the covers to her chest. Was he gone, or in the bathroom?

"Cade?" She cocked her head to one side, listening. "Cade, are you in there?"

When there was no answer, she slid out of bed, grabbed a change of underwear and her dress and then, not wanting to be caught in her nightgown in case he returned, she hurried into the bathroom and locked the door.

When she emerged thirty minutes later, he still hadn't returned. Wondering where he'd gone off to, she picked up her handbag, checked her hair and makeup in the mirror one last time, and left the room.

Downstairs, she checked the conference schedule. She had already missed half a dozen workshops. She stood there, tapping one foot, while she tried to decide if she wanted to listen to a panel of romance writers discuss "Expanding the Romance Market" more than she wanted breakfast. The panel was over at noon. Lunch was from twelve-thirty until two. There were no other workshops scheduled after lunch. The literacy signing was from two-thirty until four-thirty. The welcome reception/cocktail party wouldn't start until seven, which gave everyone plenty of time to relax and put on their party clothes.

Deciding there was no point in attending the panel since she had already missed half of it, Callie made her way to the café.

She nodded to several romance writers she passed along the way, smiled at a handsome hunk who was no doubt entered in the cover-model contest.

She ordered orange juice, coffee and a bran muffin for breakfast. Sipping her coffee, she wondered again where Cade was. Maybe he had decided to go back home.

Leaving the café, she walked back to the lobby. Several writers were gathered together, sitting around a table, and she went over to say hello. Drawing closer, she saw several of her good friends were there as well.

"Hey, girlfriend, I was wondering where you were," Vicki said as Callie sat down beside her.

Callie had known Vicki for years and had always been a little jealous of her gorgeous blond hair, deep blue eyes and long shapely legs. People often thought Vicki was one of the cover models.

"You should have come on the plane with us," Kim remarked. "We had a great time." Kim was the oldest in their crowd. She had long black hair, blue eyes, and was happily divorced.

"She'll never get on a plane," Jackie said with an exaggerated sigh. Jackie was cute and perky, with short, dark brown hair and hazel eyes. She was married to her high school sweetheart, and they had three adorable little girls, ages seven, five and three. Jackie considered every conference a vacation.

"That's right," Callie agreed. For once, she was glad she was afraid to fly. If she had taken a plane with the others, she never would have met Cade.

As always when writers got together, they discussed copy edits, editors, and galleys, congratulated each other on new contracts or contests won. There was talk of the market, what was hot, what was not, whether clinch covers were better than hearts and flowers, if cartoon covers were a thing of the past.

Callie glanced at her watch. Almost twelve-thirty and still no sign of Cade.

She was laughing at something one of the girls said when she happened to glance out the window. A number of cover models, both male and female, were lounging around the pool. They were all surrounded by women wanting autographs and pictures, but the man who had drawn the biggest crowd was none other than Cade Kills Thunder.

Callie stood so she could get a better look at him, though all she could really see was his head towering above the rest. Until there was a break in the crowd, giving her a clear view of Cade. He was clad in a pair of black trunks. A white towel was draped over his shoulder. Both emphasized his dark skin.

He glanced her way then, and she quickly sat down, embarrassed at having been caught ogling him like every other female present.

Callie was pretending to be involved in the conversation at the table when she felt a hand on her shoulder.

"Hey, sleepyhead. About time you woke up." All conversation around them stopped as every female eye swung in Cade's direction.

Kim poked Callie in the ribs. "Callie, who's this?" she asked, smiling at Cade.

"Oh, I'm sorry. Kim, this is Cade Kills Thunder. Cade, this is Kim Nethercott, Hilda Jensen, Jackie Patterson, Vicki Brown, Marian Lewis and Helen Kelly."

"Pleased to meet you, ladies," he replied easily, then looked at Callie again. "I'm going to go change, and then we'll grab some lunch, okay?"

Aware that she was now the center of attention, Callie nodded. "Okay."

As soon as he was out of earshot, the inevitable questions began.

"Who is he?"

"Where did you meet him?"

"Is he one of the models?"

"Is he married?"

"Is he straight?"

Callie laughed. "He's just an acquaintance. He picked me up on the side of the road. He isn't a model." *Yet.* "He's not married." *And not likely to be anytime soon.* "And yes, he's straight."

And so saying, she left them all standing there gawking after her. She couldn't help smiling. For the first time in her life, she had shown up at a conference with a man, and not just *any* man, but the best-looking man in the whole darn place.

Cade was a man who liked women and he knew they liked him, but never in all his life had he been the center of so much feminine attention in one day. Before he made it back to his room, he'd been stared at, sized up, whistled at five times and propositioned twice.

When he reached his room, he closed and locked the door, and then grinned. He felt like a stud horse in a field of fillies, and they were all in season.

When he stripped off his trunks, a folded piece of paper fluttered to the floor. Picking it up, he unfolded it and frowned. There was nothing written on it but a room number.

Grinning, he dropped the paper in the trash can in the bath-room, then took a quick shower, dried his hair and pulled on a pair of clean jeans, a shirt and his boots.

He passed a couple of men on his way to the lobby. Judg-ing by the number of women who flocked around them, many taking pictures or getting autographs, he figured the men were either movie stars or cover models.

With a shake of his head, he threaded his way through the crowd.

A pretty young woman with curly brown hair stepped in front of him, blocking his path. "Are you anyone?"

"'Fraid not."

"Are you sure?"

"Pretty sure."

She looked momentarily disappointed, then shrugged. "Well, would you mind if I took your picture anyway?" She stared up at him, her expression hopeful.

He hesitated a moment, then said, "No, I guess not."

Uttering a little squeal of excitement, she fished a dispos-able camera out of a large tote bag. The words So Many Books, So Little Time was emblazoned on one side of the bag. Scattered around the printed words were autographs of vari-ous authors.

Several other women gathered around. He heard whispers of "Who's he?" and "Isn't that John DeSalvo?"

Three or four other women produced cameras and pretty soon he was the center of a large crowd of women, all hap-pily snapping his picture and asking him to "look this way and smile."

"There you are!"

Glancing over his shoulder, Cade saw Callie weaving her way through the crowd.

"Excuse me, ladies," she said, taking Cade by the arm, "but he's with me, and we're late for lunch."

Cameras continued to flash as she led him away.

"Thanks for rescuing me," Cade said, grinning. "I was beginning to feel like the last piece of chocolate in the box."

"Very funny," she said dryly.

Chuckling, Cade opened the door for her and followed her into the restaurant. A moment later, they were seated at a table in the back.

Callie couldn't help noticing that every woman over the age of puberty, from the hostess to their waitress to the patrons, stared at Cade as if he was, indeed, the last piece of chocolate in the box. It filled her with a rare sense of feminine satisfaction to know that she was the envy of every female who saw her in his company.

Of course, she couldn't help staring at him, either. He wore a pair of jeans, a dark blue plaid Western shirt and boots. She was certain he wouldn't have looked more handsome if he had been wearing an Armani suit and Gucci loafers. She loved the warm rich bronze of his skin, the deep brown of his eyes, the slight cleft in his chin. And his hair…every time she looked at it, she wanted to run her fingers through the thick black strands…

She felt a rush of heat in her cheeks when she realized he was watching her, one brow raised in wry amusement.

"Not you, too," he muttered.

"I don't know what you're talking about," she said with an aggrieved sniff.

"Uh-huh."

She was grateful for the arrival of the waitress. She ordered a Caesar salad and a glass of iced tea, grimaced as Cade ordered a steak, rare, with all the trimmings, and a cup of coffee, black.

"So, what's this literacy signing you're supposed to be doing?" he asked.

"It's for charity. Most of the authors here are involved. Readers buy books and the authors sign them, and the proceeds benefit the literacy foundation. It's very worthwhile."

Cade grunted softly. He couldn't remember the last time he had read a book that hadn't had something to do with running a ranch or the cattle business. He read the paper, of course, and some other publications but, again, they all had to do with horses or cattle.

Their order arrived a few minutes later.

So did Kim and Jackie and Vicki, ostensibly to remind Callie that she was supposed to be at her seat in the meeting room half an hour before the signing started.

"Thanks for the reminder," Callie replied drily.

Cade rose to his feet. "Will you ladies join us?"

"They can't," Callie said quickly.

"That's too bad," Cade said, resuming his seat. "Maybe another time."

"Count on it," Vicki purred, winking at him.

"Definitely," Kim added, dragging her hand over Cade's shoulder before she turned and followed the others.

Callie blew out a breath as she watched her friends leave.

"What was that all about?" Cade asked.

"As if you didn't know." Stabbing the lettuce with her fork, she took a bite.

Smothering a grin, Cade cut into his steak. Unless he missed his guess, Red was a little jealous. He wasn't sure why that pleased him so much, but it did. "So, what's on the agenda after the book signing?"

"There's a welcome reception tonight, nothing fancy. I hope you'll come. Tomorrow after lunch is the cover-model pageant."

"Whoa now. What's that?"

"Well, one of the romance magazines runs a contest every year and readers send in pictures of men they know that they think would make good cover models. The winner will be picked tomorrow night during the costume ball."

He grunted softly. "Think I'll take in a movie."

"Oh."

"You got a problem with that?"

"Well, I was hoping…"

Cade picked up his coffee cup. She blushed easily, he thought. It was kind of cute. "What were you hoping?"

"That you'd be my date, at lunch tomorrow." She pushed the salad around on her plate. "And at dinner tomorrow night."

"I don't have anything to wear to a costume ball. And how fancy is lunch?"

"Lunch is pretty casual. Just jeans and a shirt is fine."

"Uh-huh." He stared at her over the rim of his cup, unable to shake the feeling that she was up to something, but for the life of him, he couldn't figure out what it was. "And tomorrow night?"

"Well, I'm dressing as Annie Oakley, but not everyone comes in costume. You can just wear your regular clothes, unless you'd like to buy something new. I'd pay for it, of course."

"Thanks, Red, but I can buy my own clothes."

"Then you'll do it? You'll be my…" She cleared her throat. "My date."

All his instincts told him to say no, but for some reason he didn't understand and was afraid to examine too closely, he couldn't refuse her. "I guess so."

"Don't forget to wear your hat. It'll be a nice touch, you know?"

"Right."

She beamed at him.

"So, what's on the agenda for Sunday?"

"The awards ceremony."

"What kind of awards?"

"Book awards. You know, best historical, best contemporary, best paranormal, best first book, that sort of thing."

"Are you in the running?"

"Yes. I need to go up and change for the signing. I'll see you later, okay?"

"Sure."

She dug in her purse and placed a ten-dollar bill on the table.

"What's that for?" he asked gruffly.

"My lunch, silly."

"Keep it."

"But…"

He picked up the ten and thrust it into her hand. "I said keep it."

Rather than make a scene, she dropped the bill into her purse. "Thank you, Cade."

He watched her walk away, wondering what the devil he'd gotten himself into, then shrugged. It was too late to worry about it now.

He finished his meal, paid the check and left the restaurant. He wandered around the hotel for a while, feeling like a rooster in a henhouse. He was beginning to wonder if there were any other men registered besides himself and a handful of cover models.

He was looking for the meeting room where they were having the book signing when two women stopped him. The younger and taller of the two looked Cade up and down, then whistled softly.

"Are you one of the models?" she asked.

"No, ma'am."

"Are you in the contest tomorrow?" asked the second woman, who looked old enough to be his grandmother.

"No, ma'am."

"Oh. That's too bad," the first one said. "We would have voted for you."

"Thanks," he said, grinning.

With a shake of his head, he continued on his way. He found the room he was looking for a few minutes later. Opening the door, he decided every woman in the hotel must be inside. The noise level was deafening. Rows and rows of tables were set up and women were clustered in front of them, all talking at once.

Feeling more than a little out of place in the midst of hundreds of women and no other men that he could see, Cade walked down the first aisle. The authors sat behind the tables. Stacks of paperback books were piled in front of each of them. As he moved down the row, he noticed that all the authors seemed to have something to give away: bookmarks, magnets, pens, pencils, candy, emery boards, book bags, coffee cups, Post-it notes. But, no matter what they were giving away, it all had one thing in common, and that was the name of the author and the title of her next book.

Cade was a little surprised to find a middle-aged man sitting at one of the tables. It had never occurred to him that men wrote romance novels. Apparently the author didn't want anyone to know he was male, since he wrote under the name of Claire Mackenzie. The women didn't seem to mind, though, and there were nine or ten of them waiting in line to talk to him and get his autograph on a book.

Cade glanced down the row. Where in tarnation was Red? He smiled and waved to a couple of her girlfriends who were also signing books.

He walked up and down a dozen aisles before he found Callie. She was sitting at the end of the row. A quick count showed there were more than thirty women standing in line waiting for her autograph. Some held tote bags filled with old books, and he wondered if they expected her to sign those as well.

Cade moved off to the side a little so he could get a look at her. She had changed into a navy-blue suit worn over some sort of bright pink, silky looking blouse. She had pinned her hair up save for one long curl that fell over her left shoulder. She looked poised and confident and professional as she nodded and smiled, posed for pictures with her fans and signed one book after another.

Cade shook his head. Hard to believe this was the same woman he had found on the side of the road only a few days ago. Knowing he would probably regret it, he moved to the back of the line.

Callie smiled and nodded as a woman in her early twenties asked her to sign a copy of her latest book.

"It's for my mother," the young woman said. "She loves your work, but she couldn't be here."

Callie opened the book to the title page. "What's her name?"

"Theresa."

Callie wrote a few words, signed her name, and handed the woman the book.

"Thank you." The woman hesitated, then said, "You don't know how much your books mean to me. When my mother was sick and in the hospital, I read your books. They helped me through a really bad time, you know. Helped me to escape my worries for a little while. That's why she couldn't be here. She's still recovering from her operation."

Touched by the woman's words, Callie reached for her hand and gave it a squeeze. "Thanks for letting me know. And tell your mother hello for me."

"I will, and thanks again."

Hugging the book to her chest as if it were a rare treasure, the woman walked away.

Without looking up, Callie reached for the next book. "Who should I make this out to?"

"Jacob."

Startled by the sound of his voice, Callie looked up. Her eyes widened in disbelief when she saw Cade standing there. "What are *you* doing here?"

Cade shrugged. "I wanted to see a real author at work." He stared after the woman who had been ahead of him. "That was—" he lifted one shoulder and let it fall "—nice, what she said. Must have made you feel good."

"Yes, it did." Lowering her voice so only he could hear, she said, "You didn't have to buy a book, you know. I would have given you one later."

"Just sign it, Red, you've got a lot of fans who are anxious to meet you."

She couldn't believe he had waited in line for her to sign a book for his great-grandfather.

She handed him the book. "Thank you."

"Thank you." He winked at her. "I'll see you tonight."

Chapter Seven

The welcome reception that night was, as Callie had said, casual. The dinner was buffet style with an open bar. Callie seemed to know just about everyone and they all came up to tell her how much they had liked her last book, how eager they were for the next one, and to wish her luck at the awards ceremony.

She introduced Cade to her agent, who seemed to be a pretty likable guy, and later to her editor. Mary Louise Kendall was a tall woman, with shoulder-length brown hair, light brown eyes and flawless skin. She wore a shimmery blue dress and high-heeled sandals. Cade thought she looked more like a fashion model than an editor, but then, what did he know about editors?

"Mary Louise, this is Cade Kills Thunder," Callie said. "You remember, I told you about him on the phone?"

Mary Louise smiled warmly at Cade as she extended her hand. "I remember," she replied. "I'm pleased to meet you."

"Cade, this is my editor, Mary Louise Kendall."

Cade nodded as he took the other woman's hand. Mary Louise had a firm grip. She seemed especially glad to meet him, though he wasn't sure why. He wondered what Callie had told her editor about him. Mary Louise looked him over from head to toe, as if he were a studhorse she was thinking of adding to her herd.

"I think you're right, Callie," Mary Louise said as she took her leave. "I'll talk to you more about it later."

After dinner, a three-piece band provided music for dancing. Cade didn't fancy himself as much of a dancer, but it gave him a good excuse to hold Callie in his arms. And she felt good there. She had changed into a sleeveless dark green sundress and a pair of matching heels that had to be four inches high. He didn't see how she could walk in the darn things, let alone dance. Even in high heels, the top of her head barely reached his shoulder.

Callie tried to concentrate on following Cade's lead but it wasn't easy. She was all too aware of his large callused hand holding hers, of his body brushing against hers, of his arm around her waist. His nearness played havoc with her senses. His woodsy aftershave lotion teased her nostrils. She was acutely aware of the strong muscles in his back as they rippled beneath her palm. His breath whispered softly over her cheek. And his eyes…they were as warm and dark as hot fudge, as intimate as a caress as he gazed down at her.

The silence made her uncomfortable and she searched her mind for something to say, but words failed her. *Come on, Callie, you're a writer. Pretend this is a scene in one of your books and write some of that witty dialogue you're famous for!*

His hand moved up and down her back.

When she shivered with pleasure, he drew her a little closer.

In spite of her high heels, she still had to look up at him. Her heart seemed to skip a beat as his gaze locked with hers.

It was a scene she had written countless times before—the heroine dancing with the tall, dark, handsome hero. If it had indeed been a scene from one of her books, he would have kissed her by now.

But this was reality and…she stared into his eyes, her heartbeat quickening as he slowly lowered his head.

And kissed her.

In this case, reality was ever so much better than fiction.

At the touch of his lips on hers, everything else fell away. The music, the people, everything but the man holding her in his embrace.

His masculine scent tantalized her. The arms around her waist were sure and strong, yet gentle. His lips were firm and warm, and when his tongue slid along her lower lip, it was the most natural thing in the world to let hers meet his. She shivered with the sheer pleasure of his touch.

She felt her cheeks flame as the sound of applause penetrated the roaring in her ears. Drawing away from Cade, she was embarrassed to find that the music had stopped and they were the only couple left on the dance floor, and that the applause was for her and Cade.

Mortified, her gaze lowered, she hurried off the dance floor. Kim and her entourage quickly surrounded her.

"Well, that was the best entertainment so far!" Kim exclaimed, her blue eyes dancing with merriment.

Callie glared at her friend. "Would you please hush!"

"Well, darlin'," Marian drawled, batting her eyelashes, "if you don't want him, just point him in my direction and I'll do the rest." She struck a pose, one hand on her hip, one finger twirling a curl of her long brown hair. "Be no trouble at all to take him off your hands."

Hilda laughed softly, her gray eyes twinkling with mirth. "Really, Callie, all this time you had us convinced you had no interest in anything but your writing. My, oh my, how times have changed."

"No kidding." Vicki ran a hand through her hair. "You sure had me fooled."

Jackie nodded. "I guess the truth is out now, isn't it?"

"Evenin', ladies."

All conversation came to an abrupt halt as Cade appeared at Callie's side. "I thought you might like a drink," he said, handing her a glass.

"Thank you." Thinking it was cranberry juice, she gulped it down and then gasped. Her insides were now as hot as her cheeks. "What was that?"

"A Sea Breeze."

"Oh!" She fanned herself with her hand. "What's in it?"

Cade shrugged. "A little vodka, a little grapefruit juice, a little cranberry juice."

Vicki grinned up at Cade. "Callie doesn't drink anything stronger than root beer."

"Is that right?" Cade patted Callie on the back. "I didn't know."

Callie thrust the glass at Cade. "I think I'm going to my room. Good night, ladies."

Head high, her cheeks still burning, Callie fled the scene for the peace and privacy of her room.

Only it wasn't private. Moments later, Cade appeared.

"Why didn't you tell me you don't drink?"

"The subject never came up."

"Well, I'm sorry. Is there anything else I should know about you?" His tone was light and teasing, but his eyes darkened as his gaze moved over her.

Feeling like a doe in the headlights, Callie shook her head.

"Come now," he said, taking a step closer. "You must have some other secrets hidden away." He lifted one brow. "I know you like taffy and chocolate. And being kissed."

She licked lips gone suddenly dry as he moved toward her. "Cade…"

"Talk to me, Red. Tell me about you. I want to know everything." He brushed his lips over hers. "Your likes." He kissed the tip of her nose. "Your dislikes." His hands folded over her shoulders, drawing her up against him.

"I…" She swallowed hard, unable to speak, unable to think when he was holding her so close, when he was looking down at her like that, his eyes filled with fire and desire.

"Do you like this?" he asked, and lowering his head, he kissed her.

She leaned into him, helpless to resist. Did she like it? Was he kidding? What was there *not* to like? Her breasts tingled where they were flattened against his hard muscular chest, her heart was beating wildly. His tongue delved into her mouth and she felt her knees go weak, knew she would have collapsed at his feet if not for his arms on her shoulders.

He drew back, his gaze searching hers. "Damn, Red," he muttered. He kissed her again, hard and quick, and then stalked out of the room.

Stunned, Callie stared after him. She felt a keen sense of disappointment because he had left but, at the same time, she was relieved that he was gone because she was very afraid of what might have happened if he had stayed.

Leaving the hotel, Cade got into his truck, drove into town, and stopped at the first bar he came to. Inside, he started to order a whiskey, then ordered a glass of orange juice instead. If there was one thing he needed right now, it was a clear head. He didn't know what had happened back there in Red's room, but whatever it was, it had jarred him right down to his socks, made him think about things that, until he had met Callie, he was sure he didn't want. Things like marriage and settling down. Yes, his parents seemed happy enough, but they were from another generation. People today seemed to get a new spouse about as often as they got a new car. Several of the guys he hung around with were married; none of them seemed particularly happy.

He frowned as he sipped his drink. Maybe he had left too soon. Maybe she wouldn't have said no and slapped his face if he had suggested they spend a little time under the sheets getting to know each other better. But even as the thought crossed his mind, he knew Red wasn't that kind of a woman. Even in this day and age of anything goes, he had a hunch that she wasn't the kind of girl to sleep around. Hell, he wouldn't be surprised to discover she was still a virgin, although she sure didn't kiss like one.

Damn. Why, out of all the women in the world, did he have to want her? The hotel was filled with women and he was pretty sure any number of them would have been happy to spend a few hours in the sack with him without wanting or expecting anything in return, including the one who had slipped him her room number.

Just his luck that Callie Walker wasn't one of them.

Finishing his drink, he left the bar and took a walk through the town, determined to give Callie plenty of time to get into bed and go to sleep.

Later, climbing back into his truck, he didn't know whether he should thank his great-grandfather for sending him on this errand or never speak to the old man again.

Callie took a quick shower, donned her nightgown and climbed into bed. And all the while she had one ear cocked toward the door, listening for Cade's return. Why had he left so abruptly? Had she done something wrong? She dismissed that notion out of hand. He had been just as caught up in that kiss as she had been, she was sure of it. So, why had he left?

Closing her eyes, she willed herself to go to sleep, but to no avail. She couldn't get Cade out of her mind, couldn't stop thinking of how right it had felt to be in his arms, the magic in his kiss.

It was after midnight when Cade returned to their room.

Lying there in the dark, her eyes tightly closed, she listened to him undress in the dark. She tried to shut out the sounds of his clothing sliding over his skin.

Did he wear boxers or briefs?

It was a question that, however foolish, kept her awake long after he had gone to bed.

Chapter Eight

In the morning, Callie woke to again find herself alone. Rising, she made a cup of coffee and sipped it leisurely before dressing and leaving the room.

She went to the café for breakfast, all the while wondering what Cade was doing. She nodded at a couple of writers she recognized. A few minutes later, her editor stopped by her table and Callie invited Mary Louise to join her.

They passed a pleasant hour together. Mary Louise told her their publishing house was thinking about launching a new line of fantasy romances and asked Callie if she would be interesting in writing for it.

"I'd love to!" she replied enthusiastically. "In fact I have an idea for a *Beauty and the Beast* story that would be perfect."

"I knew we could count on you. How about sending me a proposal?"

"I'll get to it as soon as I get back home."

"Great! We'd love to have you do the launch book for the series."

Callie nodded, thrilled to have been asked. As much as she loved writing historicals, she was getting a little tired of the Old West. This would give her a chance to explore something new and maybe pick up some new readers along the way.

"I can't wait to see what you come up with," Mary Louise said. "Have your agent call me and we'll get started on a contract."

"Will do."

"Good. Listen, I've got to go. I've got an interview with a wannabe."

"All right. See ya later."

"So long, sweetie." Rising, Mary Louise picked up the check. "It's on me this time."

"Thanks, Mary Louise."

Callie couldn't stop smiling. It was a real coup to be asked to write the first book in a new line. She couldn't wait until it was official so she could tell the girls. Finishing her coffee, she left the restaurant.

When she entered the lobby a few minutes later, she wasn't the least bit surprised to find that Cade was the center of attention. At least two dozen women were gathered around him, including Vicki, Jackie and Helen. Callie moved up behind the crowd, curious to see what was going on. Her jaw dropped when she saw that he was having his picture taken with one woman after another, and that he was also signing autographs.

"Amazing," she murmured.

"Isn't it?" Kim remarked, coming to stand beside her. "You should have entered him in the cover-model contest. I'll bet he would have won hands down."

"I think you're right," Callie replied drily. "And speaking of covers, Mary Louise thinks he'd be perfect for the cover of my next book."

"Really? That's great."

"Well, I'm not sure he'll think so." Callie scowled when a woman put her arm around Cade's waist and smiled for the camera. "Then again, maybe he will. He doesn't seem to be the least bit shy."

"Have you talked to him about doing your cover?"

"No, not yet. I was going to wait until we're on our way back to his place."

"This just keeps getting better and better. So, where'd you meet him, anyway?"

"She said he picked her up on the side of the road," Marian recalled, coming up behind them. "Is that true, Callie?"

Callie glared at Marian. "Yes, but not the way you're obviously thinking. Anyway, it's a long story. Isn't there a workshop you should be attending?"

"Please!" Marian said, rolling her eyes. "I never go to those things."

"Hey, girls, what's going on?" Hilda asked.

"Nothing."

"We were just watching the floor show," Kim said.

Hilda glanced at the crowd, and then grinned. "We should have sold tickets. It would have paid our conference fees."

"Well," Kim said, glancing at her watch, "As much as I hate to, I've got to go. I've got an appointment with my editor."

"And I've got an appointment to get my hair done," Marian said.

"We're all sitting together at lunch, right?" Hilda asked.

Callie nodded.

"Will he be there, too?" Marian asked.

"Yes," Callie said. "So behave yourselves."

"Not to worry, dear," Kim said, stifling a grin.

Somehow, Callie wasn't reassured.

Left alone, she made her way through the crowd. She wasn't sure, but she thought Cade's cheeks flushed a bit when he looked up and saw her standing with the others.

"Hey, Red."

"Hey, yourself." She glanced around. "Holding court, are you?"

Cade shrugged. "They just sort of wandered over and start-ing, taking pictures." He smiled for the next woman in line, who quickly snapped several photos. "I told them I'm nobody, but they don't seem to care."

She had no trouble believing that. What woman in her right mind wouldn't find him attractive? "Well, I'm going to go relax by the pool for a while. I'll see you at lunch."

"Red, wait." He quickly signed an autograph for the next woman in line, then held up his hands. "Sorry, ladies, I've got to go."

"Are you sure you can drag yourself away?" Callie asked testily. "You don't have to leave on my account."

"You mad about something?" he asked, falling into step beside her.

"Why should I be mad?"

"I don't know. You tell me."

"Don't be ridiculous. I'm not mad. I just don't want to spoil your fun."

Laughing, he opened the door for her, then followed her into the pool area.

Stung by his laughter, Callie sat down in a chair under an umbrella.

Cade sat down beside her. "So, what time's lunch?"

"Twelve-thirty."

"I've never been to a cover-model pageant before."

"I doubt you'll find it very interesting. They're all men."

"Too bad."

She looked him over from head to foot. "You should be one of them," she muttered.

"What?"

"Nothing."

"Tell me you didn't say what I thought I heard."

"Why are you so surprised? Every woman here is think-ing the same thing." She felt a twinge of guilt. She was al-ways getting letters from readers asking why she didn't have a real Indian on her covers. She had hoped Cade would change that. What would he say when she told him that she had suggested that very thing to her editor and that Mary Louise had been so enthusiastic that she was already planning to use Cade on the cover of Callie's next historical?

"Me, a model?" Cade shook his head emphatically. "No way."

"Yes way," she retorted.

He laughed again, then settled back in the lounge chair. "So, do you go to these things often?"

"I try to do one a year. It's a good way to keep in touch with my readers, find out what they thought of my last book. You know, stuff like that."

"So, do you get fan letters, too?"

"Yes. But most of it is e-mail these days."

"Do you answer them?"

"Of course. If someone takes the time to write, they deserve an answer. One of my favorite letters was from a young mother of three who said she'd never cared for reading and that the only thing she read was the newspaper until she saw my last book in the grocery store and bought it. She said she loved it and couldn't wait to read another one."

"You ever get mail from guys?"

"Yes, from time to time." She didn't mention that some of them were inmates. "One of my favorite letters was from a young Lakota boy who said my books gave him a new appreciation for his heritage. That really touched me. I had another letter from a Cherokee lady who said that after reading one of my books, she decided to do her genealogy and learn more about her people and her family."

Callie grinned. "And then there was a letter from a lady who said she read one of my books and didn't like it. She said her husband read it and he didn't like it either. I had the feeling she wanted her money back. I probably would have sent it to her if Kim hadn't talked me out of it."

"Maybe I'll have to read one."

As always, the thought of someone she knew reading one of her books made her nervous. She remembered telling one of her friends that it made her feel like she was standing outside, naked, for the whole world to see.

Callie glanced at her watch. "We should go. I'm supposed to save a table for the girls."

They found a table near the front. The hotel had done a nice job of decorating. The cloths were dark blue linen, the napkins were white. The flowers in the center of the table were red, white and blue carnations.

A long table at the front of the room was reserved for the models.

A makeshift runway had been set up for the pageant.

The room began to fill a few minutes later and soon the air was filled with the sound of conversation and laughter.

Kim and the others arrived and they all hugged each other as if they hadn't seen each other in days instead of hours.

The president of the local writers' chapter welcomed everyone and thanked those who had helped to make the conference a success. Then lunch was served.

Cade was a man who loved women, all women, but this was the first time he'd been at a table with this many women who weren't related to him. It was quite an experience, especially when the writers began discussing love scenes and whether readers preferred long drawn-out, graphic love scenes, fade to black or something in between. From there, the discussion turned to how much description was too much, finding inventive ways to describe what went on between a man and a woman, how far was too far and at what point a love scene stopped being romance and turned into erotica.

Kim looked over at him, her eyes alight with mischief. "What do you think, Cade? How much is too much?"

He held up both hands in a gesture of surrender. "Oh, no, you're not getting me into this."

"Chicken," Vicki said, laughing.

"Darn right, although…" His gaze settled on Callie's face. "I've always wondered where romance writers get their ideas. Red, here, says she does a lot of research for her books. I was wondering if that included the love scenes."

Callie stared at him, feeling as though her face was suddenly on fire.

"Yes, Callie," Marian said, grinning. "Do tell."

She was saved from having to answer when a lady stepped to the microphone and announced the cover-model pageant was about to begin.

One by one, the hopefuls walked out on the runway. They were all handsome and buff, and they all wore costumes of one kind or another. Abbreviated costumes. One man was a knight, another a barbarian. There was a fireman and a police officer, a doctor and a lion tamer.

The women in the audience cheered and whistled for their favorites.

"And now, for the first time that I can recall," the emcee said, "we have a write-in candidate. Cade Kills Thunder."

Cade's dark eyes narrowed as he turned to look at Callie. "You didn't," he said, his voice thick with accusation. "Tell me you didn't."

"I didn't. Honest."

"Go on up," Kim said, tugging on Cade's shirtsleeve. "They're waiting for you."

"Cade. Cade. Cade." The women in the audience took up the cry.

"You'd better go before they come and get you," Helen said, grinning.

Teeth clenched, Cade pushed away from the table and stalked to the runway. Whistles and catcalls followed him.

The emcee smiled at the audience. "Ladies, I applaud your good taste."

"His shirt," called a woman from the front of the crowd. "Tell him to take off his shirt."

The emcee looked over at Cade. "Do you mind? You could refuse, of course, but I wouldn't want to be responsible for what might happen."

Grimacing, Cade shrugged out of his long-sleeved Western shirt and tossed it aside. He wasn't wearing a T-shirt underneath. Lamplight played over his bare chest and broad shoulders.

More whistles and catcalls filled the air.

"He's never going to forgive me for this," Callie muttered.

But no one was listening. As though spellbound, they were all staring at Cade. And so was she.

"All right, ladies," the emcee said drily. "I think we've all had a good look. The winner will be announced tonight during the costume ball."

"He's never going to forgive me for this," Callie said again. "Never in a million years."

Chapter Nine

As Cade grabbed his shirt and pulled it on, he didn't know if he was angry or flattered or just flat-out embarrassed. It was one thing to know women found him attractive and another to have them screaming and hollering for him to take his shirt off.

Surrounded by women—some young enough to be his daughter, some old enough to be his grandmother—he left the runway, tucking in his shirttail as he went. He had a few choice things to say to Miss Callie Walker. Things that couldn't be said in a room full of women.

Smiling, nodding, and shaking hands with those who promised to vote for him, he finally made his way back to the table.

Callie was noticeably absent.

Cade looked at Kim. "Where is she?"

"Hiding, I think."

"Smart girl."

Marian laughed. "She didn't have anything to do with it, honest."

"Then why isn't she here?"

"If you could see the look on your face, you'd know why," Helen said, grinning.

"We're on our way to a workshop," Hilda said. "You're welcome to come along. It's on writing the male point of view."

"Thanks," Cade said drily, "but I don't think so."

The women rose and gathered their belongings.

"We'll see you tonight then," Kim said.

"Don't count on it."

Vicki looked up at him, one brow arched. "What's the matter, Cade? Afraid you'll lose?"

He shook his head. "No way, honey. I'm afraid I'll win."

They all laughed at that.

"Well, see you later," Kim said, and followed the others out of the room.

Seeing several women headed toward him, Cade pivoted on his heel and escaped out a side door.

Where would she go? Their room was the obvious place, which was why he was pretty sure she wouldn't go there. If she really wanted to avoid him, the best place to do it was in one of those silly workshops. Figuring that that was where she was, he went to their room and changed into his trunks and headed for the pool to cool off.

It wasn't as crowded as he'd feared it might be. There were a few young mothers watching over their kids at the shallow end, and a few older women stretched out on lounge chairs, their noses stuck in the free hardcover books that one of the publishers had been handing out at the literary signing.

With a sigh of relief, he walked toward the deep end of the pool. His gaze was drawn to the woman poised on the diving board. He started at her ankles and slowly worked his way up. She had great legs. Not long, but great just the same. She wasn't runway model skinny, but the body encased in a dark blue one-piece bathing suit went in and out in all the right places. Long red hair fell over one shoulder…

He felt a sharp jolt of awareness when he realized it was Callie.

Ignorant of his presence, she executed a beautiful back flip, then swam toward the edge of the pool.

He was waiting there, one hand extended to help her out of the water, when she reached the side.

Her eyes widened when she saw him. "Are you here to help me out," she asked warily, "or drown me?"

"I thought about drowning you," he replied, "but there are too many witnesses right now."

Reaching for his hand, she let him help her out of the pool, then retrieved her towel from the back of a chair where she'd left it and wrapped it around her hair, turban-style. "I didn't have anything to do with it," she said. "Honest."

"Why don't I believe you?"

"I don't know." She sat down at one of the tables. "Why don't you?"

He sat down across from her, his gaze intent upon her face.

It was all Callie could do to keep from fidgeting. Even though she hadn't entered his name in the contest, she had talked to her editor about the possibility of using Cade on her next cover. And after today, there could be no doubt that, with Cade on the cover, even women who didn't care for her writing style would probably buy the book just because his image was on the front. And she couldn't blame them. From time to time, she had bought books she had no intention of reading simply because of the hunk on the cover.

"You'd make a great model," she blurted, unnerved by his silence.

"Forget it!" he said sharply, and then frowned. "You're hiding something. What is it?"

"Nothing."

"Come on, Red, what's going on in that pretty little head of yours?"

"Nothing! I…why are you so against it?"

"So it *was* your idea?"

"No! But…well."

"But what?" His voice was hard and flat, his eyes like flint.

Might as well say it and get it over with. "The first time I saw you, I knew you'd be perfect for the cover of my next book. And my editor thinks so, too."

"Is that right?"

She nodded. "Mary Louise pictured you on a white horse, a feather in your hair, a streak of black paint on one cheek and another across your chest." She spoke in a rush, wanting to get it all said. "And you'd be carrying a feathered lance. It would make a striking cover."

Rising, Cade stood looking down at her, his eyes narrowed. "Well, forget it, honey," he drawled, "'cause it ain't gonna happen."

"If you'd just…"

He shook his head. "It's not gonna happen, Red. Not in this life, or any other." And so saying, he stalked away from the table.

She couldn't help noticing that every female head in the vicinity turned to follow him.

Muttering under his breath, Cade went in search of a drink. So, that had been her plan all along, had it? To turn him into a cover model. Of all the harebrained ideas he'd ever heard in his life, that had to be the worst. He'd seen the guys on those covers, muscles pumped up and bulging as they bent some half-dressed female over their arms. He'd be the laughingstock of every truck driver he knew if he were fool enough to let himself be talked into doing such a ridiculous thing.

Damn!

No wonder Red had been so sweet and agreeable all this time. He wouldn't be at all surprised to learn she had called the garage in Dillon and asked them to make up some story about her car not being ready in hopes that he'd offer to drive her to Jackson. Hell, maybe the old man was in on it, too.

He ordered a beer and carried it to a table in the back of the room. Did she really expect him to go back to the hotel tonight?

He swore softly, remembering that he was supposed to be her date for the costume ball. Well, she could just find someone else…

He didn't like the idea of another man escorting her either.

Sitting back in his chair, he closed his eyes. And saw her standing on the diving board, her long red hair like a shimmering fall of fire over her shoulder, the blue bathing suit perfectly outlining her curvy figure.

As angry as he was, he couldn't stand her up at the last minute. He had been brought up better than that. He'd promised to be her date so he would take her to the dance, but that didn't mean he had to dance with her. Let some other sucker waltz her around the floor, he thought irritably, but then he remembered how good she had felt in his arms the night before—the silky feel of her hair against his cheek, the way her curvy little body had fit against his, all warm and soft, the intoxicating taste of her lips…

He swore again. It was going to be a hell of a long night and a long ride home.

Callie was in their room when Cade showed up a couple of hours later. She looked mighty cute in her Annie Oakley getup. The skirt, which was short and red and fringed along the bottom, showed off her legs. She wore a white blouse and a red vest that matched the skirt. A black leather holster was slung around her hips. A white cowboy hat sat on the dresser.

She blushed as his gaze moved over her.

She watched him warily as he gathered up a change of clothes and headed into the bathroom. "Should I wait for you?"

"If you want." He didn't wait for an answer. Going into the bathroom, he closed the door. He knew he was being a jerk, but he couldn't seem to help himself.

The bathroom smelled of hair spray and perfume. Undressing, he stepped into the shower and turned the water on full blast. Upset with her or not, all he really wanted to do was pull her into the shower with him, then spend the rest of the night making love to her.

Gritting his teeth, he turned off the hot water, hoping a cold shower would cool him off and clear his head. It didn't help.

Callie paced the floor. She knew Cade was angry with her. She had expected him to refuse to go with her tonight. To tell the truth, she wasn't sure she wanted him to go with her now.

She glanced at the bathroom door, trying not to imagine him in the shower. It was useless. He had a great body, long and lean and bronze. And he had great arms. She'd always had a weakness for men with broad shoulders and tanned muscular arms.

With a sigh, she went to stand at the window, trying not to remember how wonderful it had been to be in those arms the night before, trying to forget how well they had danced together, trying to forget how he'd made her feel, as if she was the most beautiful and desirable woman in the room.

She wished suddenly that they had never come here. More than anything, she wanted a chance to get to know him better, to spend time with him on his ranch. That wasn't likely to happen now, she thought ruefully. She'd be surprised if he were willing to drive her back to Dillon.

She tensed as the shower went off.

He emerged from the bathroom a few minutes later. Lord,

but he was the most handsome man she had ever seen. He wore a pair of black jeans, a white shirt, and a supple black leather vest. His hair—hair any woman would envy—was still damp from the shower.

Siting on the edge of the bed, he pulled on a pair of socks and his boots. "Ready?" he asked curtly.

With a nod, she plucked her hat from the dresser and settled it on her head, with the brim slightly tilted down over one eye.

Grabbing his own hat from the back of a chair, he followed her out of the room.

The lobby looked like a Halloween party as ghosts, vampires and warlocks mingled with angels, fairies and elves.

Vicki was dressed as Scarlett O'Hara. Kim was the Wicked Queen from *Snow White and the Seven Dwarfs*. She carried a small gold box, which, when opened, revealed a red candy heart. Helen had decided on Joan of Arc, Hilda was a lady in waiting, Jackie was Betty Boop, and Marian was the Bride of Frankenstein, complete with big hair streaked with two white stripes.

Cade stood back as the women oohed and aahed over each other's costumes. He had to admit they all looked pretty good, but it was Callie who drew his eye again and again. In spite of everything, he wanted nothing more than to haul her back to their room and spend the rest of the night making love to her.

He trailed after the women as they made their way to the conference hall. The room was already crowded. Just about everyone was in costume. He saw several reporters wandering around, talking to readers and writers alike. Photographers were taking pictures of the models posing with fans.

They found the table reserved for them and sat down. A short time later, dinner was served. Cade listened idly to their conversation while he ate. Again, most of it was about the business of publishing. There was some gossip about an editor at one of the more prestigious houses who was rumored to be dating one of his authors, some speculation on just how much of an advance a certain well-known writer had received for her last contract, and whether one of the major publishers was about to go belly up.

A hum ran through the room as dessert was served. The wait to see which contestant would be the winner of the cover-model contest was almost over.

Callie's editor, Mary Louise Kendall, stepped up to the microphone and reminded everyone that the winner of the contest would grace the cover of Callie Walker's next historical romance.

Mary Louise held up a large white envelope. There was an air of intense anticipation as she opened it. And smiled. "And the winner is…"

Cade clenched his fists.

Callie held her breath.

"Cade Kills Thunder."

He swore under his breath as the room erupted with applause.

"Callie, would you please escort Cade to the stand?"

Cade glared at Callie. It was in his mind to refuse, but even as angry as he was, he didn't want to embarrass her in front of her friends and co-workers. Pasting a smile on his face, he stood and offered her his hand.

There was more applause. A photographer took pictures as they made their way to the podium.

Mary Louise handed him an envelope. "You'll find a plane ticket to New York City inside," she said, smiling. "Please call me as soon as you get back home and we'll set a date for the shoot and make reservations for a hotel. Congratulations."

Slipping the envelope into his back pocket, he muttered his thanks.

Mary Louise turned toward Callie. "Would you like to say a few words?"

"Just that I'm very pleased that Cade will be on my next book. I know my fans will be as thrilled as I am when they see him."

There was another round of applause and more photographs.

"It's easy to see the fans are looking forward to it just as much as you are," Mary Louise said as the applause died down. "I'll be talking to you both soon."

There was more applause, then Cade took Callie's hand and they returned to their table.

He had barely resumed his seat when he was surrounded by women with cameras, all wanting to take his photo or have their picture taken with him. They hugged him and congratulated him. A few slipped him their room numbers.

When he saw a newspaper reporter and a photographer headed his way, he excused himself and headed for the door.

Outside, he moved into the shadows, then took a deep breath. It would be a cold day in hell before he used that plane ticket.

"Cade?"

He turned to find Callie standing behind him.

"Thank you for playing along."

He grunted softly.

"I'll tell my editor you're not interested and we'll find someone else for the cover."

He nodded.

"You don't have to stick around if you don't want to. Vicki said she'd be glad to drive me back to Dillon to pick up my car."

"Are you all right with that?"

"Yes."

He stared down at her, wondering what she would do if he dragged her into his arms and took her home with him. And then he berated himself for being a fool. If she had been remotely interested in anything like that, she wouldn't have already found another ride home.

"Then I guess I'll be on my way." Taking the envelope from his back pocket, he thrust it into her hand. "Tell your editor thanks, but no thanks."

She nodded as her fingers curled around the envelope. "Goodbye, Cade."

"So long, Red."

It didn't take him long to pack his gear. Twenty minutes later, he was on the road heading for the peace and quiet of home.

For a minute there, he had thought she was going to ask him to stay.

For a minute there, he had been sorry to leave. But it was better this way. Six months on the ranch, and Red would be crying to go back to the bright lights and big city. And he sure as hell wasn't cut out for living in New York or Los Angeles. What man in his right mind would give up blue skies and rolling prairie for city smog and asphalt? He loved the ranch, loved driving and the freedom of the open road too much to give it all up...but he was sure as hell gonna miss that little redhead.

Chapter Ten

Callie stared after Cade as his long legs carried him out of her sight and out of her life. Even though it had been her idea, she couldn't believe he had left her, just like that.

Feeling heavy-hearted, she went back to the banquet room but as far as she was concerned, the evening was ruined. She had been looking forward to dancing with Cade again, to having his arms around her. Now he was gone and she would never see him again.

Vicki and the others tried to cheer her up and it worked for a little while. But later, back in her room, she sat on the edge of the bed fighting the urge to cry. For the first time in months, she had found a man she was attracted to and she'd made a mess of things. Of course, it hadn't all been her fault. True, she had talked to Mary Louise, but she hadn't had anything to do with the cover-model fiasco. Thinking about it now, she found it odd that Cade had been so upset. The man loved women, there was no doubt of that, and no doubt that they loved him! But she really couldn't blame him for being turned off by all the attention. She was basically shy and sometimes the attention she received at book signings embarrassed her. Had Cade been embarrassed to be the center of so much feminine attention? She found that hard to believe, but she supposed it was possible.

She blew out a sigh. None of it mattered now. He was gone and that was that. One more day and she would be on her way back home, where she belonged. No more women asking for her autograph. No more costumes. No more big Montana skies. No more big Montana cowboys. It would be business as usual again, just her and her computer.

She packed and then went to bed, only to lie there, wide awake, reliving every moment she had spent with Cade. She had been a fool to think anything would come of their chance encounter. After all, he was a cowboy and she was a city girl. He drove a big rig and she sat in front of a computer all day. He was used to blue skies and the bawling of cattle. She was used to air you could see and taste and the sound of traffic. They were like oil and water, she mused, and not likely to mix.

But, romantic that she was, she couldn't help thinking of, and grieving for, what might have been.

In the morning, she showered and dressed, then packed her makeup and blow-dryer and checked out of her room.

She joined Vicki and Helen and the others for coffee and then went to the last workshop of the day, which was a panel of senior editors from various publishing houses. It was a question-and-answer session and while Callie did her best to pay attention, her thoughts kept wandering to Cade. She wondered if he had driven straight home or spent the night in a motel somewhere, and if he was going to stay at the ranch for a while or go back out on the road right away. She wondered how much it was going to cost to fix her car and if she dared stop at the ranch on her way home. She immediately dismissed that notion. She had no good reason to stop at the ranch and she wasn't about to make one up. He would see right through whatever ruse she used anyway, and it would just embarrass both of them.

When the workshop was over, they went to the awards ceremony, which was the last event of the conference.

The air was filled with excitement. Callie's publisher had entered her last historical in the contest and Callie accepted good wishes from several writing acquaintances and readers.

"These things make me so nervous," Hilda said, fanning herself, "I don't know why I enter. I never win."

"Maybe this will be your year," Marian said. "Think positively."

"I'm positive I won't win."

"Stop that, Hildy!" Jackie said. "You've got as good a chance as anyone."

There were numerous awards—Best First Book, Best Historical set in the United States, Best Historical set in England, Best Regency, Best Young Adult, Best Paranormal, the list went on and on.

Callie applauded the winners and was genuinely thrilled when Hilda's book won for Best Young Adult Book of the Year.

And then the emcee read the list of finalists for the Best Historical Novel set in the United States. Callie crossed her fingers and closed her eyes as the emcee began to read the names of the runner-ups. Her heart pounded harder as the names of the other four finalists were announced, and her name had not yet been called.

"And the winner is Callie Walker, for *Divided Hearts*."

Callie opened her eyes and glanced over at Vicki. "She did call my name, right? I didn't imagine it?"

"Right, silly, get on up there!"

Rising, Callie threaded her way through the tables to the podium. She had been so certain she didn't have a chance of winning that she hadn't taken the time to write an acceptance speech.

Standing in front of the microphone, the coveted statue clasped in her hands, she thanked the judges, her readers and her editor, and all the while she wished Cade was there to share the moment with her. A final thank-you to her editor and the judges, and she went back to her seat.

The rest of the program passed in a blur. There was a flurry of goodbyes, some last-minute picture-taking and promises to stay in touch. She was about to follow Vicki out of the room when she saw Cade striding toward her. She thought she was imagining things, but there was no mistaking him for anyone else. He stood head and shoulders above everyone else in the room.

Her heart seemed to stop a moment as her gaze moved over him. As usual, he was dressed in jeans and a Western shirt. She had never been happier to see anybody in her life. But she couldn't help wondering what he was doing there.

"Congratulations," he said.

"You were here?"

"Yep. Saw the whole thing. Are you ready to go?"

"Yes, but I thought…"

"Hi, Cade," Vicki said. "Nice to see you again. Callie, I'll meet you out front, okay?"

"She's going home with me," Cade said.

Vicki looked at Callie, one brow raised. "Is that right, girl-friend?"

Callie glanced from Vicki to Cade and back again. "I don't know."

"I know." Cade took Callie's hand in his. "Let's go get your bags."

"Call me when you get home," Vicki said, grinning.

"I will," Callie promised. She looked up at Cade as they made their way through the crowd to the lobby. "I thought you left."

"Yeah, well." He shrugged. "I changed my mind."

"About everything?" she asked hopefully. In her mind's

eye, she could already picture him on the cover of her next book, his long black hair falling over his shoulders, his bare chest glistening in the sunlight.

"No, Red, just about driving you back to Dillon."

Her disappointment was almost physical. He would be so perfect for the cover of her book. Why did he have to be so darn stubborn?

"You might like modeling," she said. "It would be a change from truck driving. Who knows, you might become the next Fabio."

"Thanks, but no thanks."

In spite of the fact that he refused to pose for her cover, she was thrilled that he had come back for her. At least she would be able to spend a little more time with him. And there was always a chance that, on the road to Dillon, she could change his mind.

Half an hour later her luggage was in the back of his truck and they were on the highway.

Awareness hummed between them. Time and again she slid a glance in his direction. More than once, she caught him looking back at her.

"So," he said after a while, "did you have a good time?"

"Yes."

"You looked really surprised when you won."

"I was."

"Why? You're a successful writer. You've probably won before."

"Yes, but I was up against some really big names this time."

"Now I'll really have to read your book," he remarked.

She felt her cheeks flush as she imagined him reading her love scenes. One thing was for certain—any scene involving kissing that she wrote from now on would be colored by the kisses she had shared with Cade.

They spoke little on the way home. Cade pulled into a gas

station to fill up the truck and get a cup of coffee when they were about halfway to the ranch. She dozed the rest of the way, waking when the truck came to a stop at the garage in Dillon.

Blinking the sleep from her eyes, she sat up and glanced around. "I don't see my car."

"Maybe it's parked in back. Stay here. I'll go talk to Walter."

Cade returned a few minutes later.

"Is my car ready?" Callie asked.

"Yeah. It's back at the ranch."

Callie frowned. "What's it doing there?"

"Seems Jacob picked it up the other day."

"Why would he do that?"

"I've got a pretty good idea."

"Well, would you mind sharing it with me?"

Cade blew out a sigh of exasperation. "I reckon he's matchmaking."

Callie's eyes widened. "Matchmaking!"

Cade nodded, his jaw clenched.

Callie looked out the window. Apparently he didn't like the idea. The thought hurt more than it should have, given that she and Cade hardly knew each other.

Switching on the ignition, Cade pulled out of the parking lot. His knuckles were white on the steering wheel.

They drove to the ranch in silence.

Cade pulled up next to her car, which looked as good as new.

Alighting from the truck, he walked around to open her door for her. His large hand swallowed hers as he helped her out of the truck.

"Thank you, Cade," she said, withdrawing her hand from his. "I'm sorry I was so much trouble."

He shrugged. "Have a safe drive home."

"Thank you."

He nodded.

"Would you mind putting my bags in the car? I need to go inside and reimburse Jacob."

"Sure."

She hurried up the steps, fighting the urge to cry. Why couldn't real life be more like her books? She didn't want to leave Cade. She didn't want to go back home. She wanted to stay here and write. She wanted Cade to pose for the covers of her books from now on—just hers. She wanted one of the happy-ever-after endings that flowed so easily from her fingertips to her computer screen.

She knocked on the door and when no one answered, she knocked again.

"Maybe he's not home," Cade said, coming up behind her. He opened the door for her, then followed her inside. "I'll see if I can find the bill. If not, I'll call Walter over at the garage."

"All right."

He waved a hand toward the sofa. "Sit down. I'll be right back."

She sat down, listening to Cade's footsteps as he walked down the hall. She heard the sound of a door opening, muffled voices, a loud hacking cough.

Cade's expression was grim when he returned.

"Is everything all right?"

"Jacob's in bed. Says he's feeling a little under the weather."

"Oh, I'm sorry to hear that." She reached into her purse and withdrew a pen and her checkbook. "How much do I owe him?"

"He says he can't remember."

"Oh." She bit down on her lower lip. "I guess you'd better call the garage."

"Yeah." Cade raked a hand through his hair. "Jacob wants to see you."

"He probably just wants to say goodbye," Callie remarked, rising. "Is it all right if I go back there?"

"Sure, he's expecting you. It's the last room on the right."

"Thank you." Wondering at his shuttered expression, she walked down the hall and stopped inside the doorway to the old man's bedroom.

"Jacob?"

"Callie, come in."

She entered the room. A quick glance showed the furnishings were Spartan—a double bed covered with a thick quilt, a chest of drawers, a rocking chair beside the window. Navajo rugs covered the floor. A feathered spear hung on the wall over the bed.

"I'm sorry you're not feeling well," Callie said, moving up beside him.

He covered his mouth and coughed.

"That doesn't sound good. Maybe you should go to the hospital."

He shook his head. "No hospitals. People go there, they don't come out."

Callie hid a grin. "Have you seen a doctor?"

"Joe White Bull has been to see me. I do not trust white doctors."

"Who's Joe White Bull?"

"Medicine man."

"Oh, well, that's good, I guess. What did he say?"

"That I needed to stay in bed for a few days."

Callie nodded. "I'm glad I got to meet you, Jacob," she said sincerely. "And I hope you feel better soon. Cade's calling the garage to see how much I owe you, and then I'll be on my way."

He shook his head weakly. "Stay."

"Excuse me?"

"I want you to stay."

"I don't think Cade would like that," she said wistfully.

Jacob caught her hand and gave it a squeeze. "What would you like?"

"I'd like to stay, but I have no reason to." No reason except Cade, but he didn't want her there.

"You write about the West," Jacob said. "About day-to-day life on a ranch. Have you ever spent any time on one?"

"No, I haven't, well, except for the time I've spent here but…"

"You should do research while you are here. Who knows when you'll be in this part of the country again."

"I write historical romances, not contemporary ones," Callie reminded him.

"Some things are still done the same. And the land is the same. Go riding. Our people were as one with their horses. Walk the land. Feel the earth beneath your feet. Listen to the song of the wind."

A prickle ran up her spine and she knew that Cade had entered the room.

Jacob squeezed her hand again, a gleam in his dark eyes. "Grandson, I've asked Callie to stay with us awhile."

"Is that right?" Cade asked.

Callie was glad Cade was standing behind her because she didn't think she wanted to see the expression on his face.

"White Bull said I need someone to look after me for a few days."

Cade grunted softly. "No problem. I can take care of…"

"You have work to do," Jacob said, cutting Cade off. "And Callie needs to do some research."

"I see."

From the tone of Cade's voice, Callie wondered if he saw something that she didn't.

Jacob looked at Callie. "It is settled then," he said, sounding suddenly tired. His eyelids fluttered down. "You will look after me, and Cade will look after you…"

She started to protest one last time and then, as Jacob's voice trailed off, she realized he had fallen asleep.

Slipping her hand from his, she slowly turned around to face Cade.

"I guess you'll be staying for a while," he said laconically.

"Yes." She forced a smile. "He wouldn't take no for an answer."

"Yeah. Well, I'll bring your bags in. You can stay in the same room you used before."

"Thank you. I know Jacob usually does the cooking for the two of you. I don't mind doing it, if it's all right with you."

"Suits me. I'll get your bags."

She followed him out of the room, then went into the living room where she paced the floor in front of the fireplace. Was he angry because she was staying? Should she have told Jacob she had to leave?

She sat down on the sofa, her fingertips tapping on the arm. How could she have refused him? She genuinely liked the old man. The word matchmaker rushed to the forefront of her mind and brought a rush of heat to her cheeks. Was that what Jacob was doing? She shrugged the thought away. If he hadn't wanted his grandson to marry a white woman, he certainly wouldn't want his great-grandson to marry one, so it couldn't be that.

Her stomach did a funny little flip-flop when the front door opened. Rising, she followed Cade up the stairs to the bedroom.

He dropped her bags at the foot of the bed. "I guess you know where everything is."

"Yes. Um, do you have a washing machine?"

"It's in the garage. Go through the side door in the kitchen. Soap's on the shelf."

"Thank you." She bit down on her lip, then blurted, "This wasn't my idea."

"I know." He looked at her a moment, muttered, "Dammit," and swept her into his arms. He kissed her once, hard and quick, and then he was gone, leaving her to stare after him, her whole body quivering.

Chapter Eleven

Cade crossed his arms on the top rail of the corral and stared out into the darkness. A coyote howled somewhere in the distance. It was a sad, lonely sound that was answered a moment later. Closer to home, a cow bawled for her calf. A horse stamped its foot. A faint breeze whispered through the leaves of the trees. They were familiar sounds. The sounds of home.

He glanced over his shoulder. His great-grandfather's room was dark, but a light burned upstairs in Callie's window and even as he watched, he saw her silhouette on the shade, imagined her slipping her nightgown over her head, brushing out the silky fall of her hair.

Damn.

"What are you planning, old man?" he muttered as he drew his gaze from Callie's window. Stupid question. He knew very well what the old man had in mind. Jacob figured all he had to do was find a way to put Callie in Cade's path often enough and nature would take its course. Well, the old man had sure as hell called that one right, Cade mused sourly.

There was no denying the attraction he felt for Callie, or the fact that it was mutual. Sparks flew between them every time they got together. Hell, it was all he could do to keep his hands off her.

He hadn't meant to kiss her tonight but he hadn't been able to help himself. And he was honest enough to admit he wanted more than kisses. A whole hell of a lot more. And Jacob knew it.

Cade looked up at the sky but the stars didn't have any answers either. The best thing he could do was just make himself scarce while she was here. He hadn't spent much time at the home place lately. This would be the perfect time to ride out on the range and take a good look at the land, check the water holes and clear the river of any debris if necessary. Check on the cattle.

If he played his cards right, he could be out of the house before she got up in the morning and stay out until after dark. The best thing to do would be to call in and see if he could pick up a load but he dismissed that idea as soon as it occurred to him. He didn't really think there was anything wrong with Jacob, but he didn't want to take any chances either. If the old man was really sick, then Cade needed to stay close to home.

Callie's light was still on when he returned to the house. What was she doing up so late, anyway? Going into the kitchen, he poured himself a cup of coffee, then sat down at the table, his legs stretched out in front of him. He heard the faint hum of the washer and dryer and figured she was waiting for her laundry to get done.

He had just poured himself a second cup of coffee when she entered the kitchen.

"Oh!" she exclaimed, her hand clutching the collar of her bathrobe. "I thought you'd gone to bed already."

"Not yet." His gaze moved over her. She had let her hair down and it fell over her shoulders in soft red waves. She was barefoot, her toes peeking out from under her robe, and he wondered why that seemed so intimate, so sexy. He liked the way she blushed under his regard.

He curled his hands into fists. It was all he could do to keep from taking her in his arms and burying his hands in the wealth of her hair, from bending her back over the kitchen table and easing the sudden ache in his groin.

As though reading his thoughts, she gave him a wide berth as she went to the side door. She opened it, stepped down into the garage, and firmly closed the door behind her.

Cade smiled faintly. The next few days should be interesting, he thought, very interesting indeed.

Callie removed her clothes from the dryer one item at a time. She shook them out, folded them carefully and placed them in a neat pile, all the while hoping that Cade would have finished his coffee and gone to bed by the time she was finished. It had unnerved her, finding him in the kitchen. It had seemed such a homey, domestic scene, him sitting at the table having a late-night cup of coffee, her in her robe doing a last load of wash before going to bed…

She swallowed hard, her body growing warm at thinking of Cade and bed in the same breath.

When she finished folding her clothes, she removed the next load from the washer and put it into the dryer.

Cade. For a moment, she closed her eyes and pictured him in her mind—all long black hair, rippling muscles, sun-bronzed skin stretched across impossibly broad shoulders and long, long legs.

She opened her eyes and fanned herself with her hand. Lordy, what that man did to her! Lordy, what she would like to do to him!

Picking up the pile of laundry, she pressed her ear to the door. Had he gone to bed? She didn't hear any noise coming from the kitchen, but that didn't mean anything. The man moved as soundlessly as hot fudge over ice cream.

She licked her lips, ran a hand over her hair, straightened her shoulders. And opened the door. The kitchen was empty. She told herself she was relieved that she wouldn't have to face him again, that she wouldn't have to look into those sinfully dark brown eyes or stand there, mesmerized by his gaze, wanting, hoping, that he would kiss her again.

With a shake of her head, she went upstairs to her bedroom to put away her laundry. But it wasn't clean underwear and blue jeans that occupied her thoughts; it was the face of Cade Kills Thunder.

It was his image that followed her to sleep when she went to bed.

She woke early after a restless night. Momentarily disoriented, she rubbed the sleep from her eyes, then glanced around the room. Of course, she was at Cade's ranch. The clock showed it was a little after seven. What time did cowboys get up in the morning?

Rising, she dressed quickly in a pair of jeans and a blouse she had washed the night before, stepped into her slippers and walked down the hall toward Cade's room. A peek inside showed his bed was empty.

The smell of fresh coffee tickled her nostrils as she entered the kitchen but the room was empty. Taking a mug from the shelf, she poured herself a cup of coffee and sipped it as she made her way to Jacob's bedroom. The door was open and she peered inside. She could barely make out the old man's form under the covers. Was he awake?

He stirred as she was about to turn away. "Callie, come in."

Stepping into the room, she crossed the floor and opened the curtains. "Good morning."

"Good morning."

"How are you feeling today?"

"Better."

"Good. Would you like something to eat?"

"I'd rather have a cup of that coffee."

"I'll get you one." She smiled at him. "Would you like some toast to go with it?"

He nodded. "And maybe an egg or two."

"All right." She started toward the door.

"And some bacon."

Callie grinned at him over her shoulder. "Anything else?"

"A little orange juice?"

"Good thing you're not hungry." Chuckling, she went into the kitchen to start breakfast.

Cade coaxed the mare across the shallow stream. She was fresh off the range and only green broke. For some reason, she was afraid of running water and it had taken almost two weeks to get her to walk across the stream the first time. She still wasn't comfortable in the water. She took a step, paused, took another and then another. He could feel the tension in each quivering muscle, but he had earned her trust with a lot of patience and gentle handling. She made it to the other side, then scrambled up the bank, blowing as if she had just run ten miles.

Leaning forward, Cade patted her neck. "Good girl."

Touching his heels to her flanks, he put the mare into a lope. It felt good to be riding across his own land again, to feel the power of the horse beneath him. The mare was fleet of foot and they raced across the grassland. Throwing his head back, Cade let loose the Lakota war cry, laughed aloud as it spooked a jackrabbit from cover. With another wild cry, Cade gave chase.

It reminded him of those summer days that he had spent on the reservation when he was a boy. Jacob had taught him how to hunt and how to swim, how to skin game, how to live off the land. He had taught him how to read the signs of the changing seasons, how to navigate by the moon and the stars, how to track deer and elk and to distinguish the tracks of one from the other. Those had been good times, Cade thought as the mare made a quick turn. Shining times.

A thrill of anticipation surged through him as the jackrabbit darted into a hole at the base of a deadfall. Cade leaned forward as the mare gathered herself for the jump. A moment later, they sailed effortlessly over the fallen log.

Cade let the mare run another mile or so and then gradually reined her to a halt. "You'll do to ride the river with," he said, pleased.

Dismounting, he scratched the mare's ears, gave her an affectionate slap on the shoulder. Holding the reins in one hand, he started walking back the way they had come, his gaze moving over the land. He saw twenty or thirty head of cattle grazing in the distance. Looking at them, he couldn't help feeling a sense of pride. Though the ranch was small, they raised some of the finest beef cattle and some of the best horses in the state.

He walked the mare for about a quarter of a mile, then swung into the saddle and headed home. The hinges on one of the barn doors needed to be replaced, there was a hole in the roof of the barn, one of the horses had lost a shoe. As much as he enjoyed riding the range, there was work to be done closer to home.

Closer to Callie.

Chapter Twelve

The next few days passed peacefully enough, although Callie sometimes thought she might scream in frustration. Ever since Cade had kissed her the night they returned to the ranch, the tension between them seemed to stretch tighter minute by minute. Every time he looked at her, every time his hand brushed hers or their bodies happened to touch, it was like being zapped by lightning. If only he would kiss her again, perhaps that would ease the need that engulfed her.

Jacob took his meals in bed, which meant it was just her and Cade sitting together at the kitchen table at breakfast and dinner. They made small talk to fill the taut silences—she told him about the book she was working on, he answered her questions about day-to-day ranch life. Cade didn't come to the house for lunch but even when he wasn't there, she was aware of his presence, knew that he was nearby. Her body quivered with longing whenever they were in the same room. And it was more than just the fact that he was amazing looking. She felt safe with him, knew that if she needed him, he would be there for her.

She found herself growing increasingly fond of Jacob Red Crow, too. He told her stories of life on the reservation and she made copious notes, filing them away for a future book that she planned to set in the plains of Dakota. When she promised to name a character after Jacob, he beamed at her as though he had just won the lottery.

Because she was genuinely interested in their way of life, Jacob told her some of the Lakota stories that had been passed down orally from generation to generation.

Jacob taught her that the Lakota believed that everything had a spirit of its own, even rocks, and that four was a sacred number. He told her about a Lakota god called *Iya,* who had a hunger that food couldn't satisfy. She wondered if that was the Indian version of a vampire. *Skan* was the god of the sky. *Tatanka* was the god of the buffalo.

Her favorite was *Wakinyan,* the thunderbird. He was a double-natured god, angry, shapeless and terrifying to see. He had two wings with many joints and huge talons, but no legs and no feet. *Wakinyan* had no mouth, but a huge beak with teeth that could rend anything. He had no throat, but his voice made thunder; he had no head, but he had one eye whose glance was lightning. *Wakinyan* used the clouds as robes to hide himself. Try as she might, Callie couldn't picture such a creature, but it was fascinating just the same.

And then there were the *Pte Oyate,* the buffalo people. The *Pte Oyate* had been created by *Skan* to do the will of *Wakan Tanka. Skan* made the buffalo people by taking something from all the other gods. From *Inyan,* the rock, he took the material for bones, from *Maka,* the earth, he made flesh, from *Unk,* the god of passion, he took blood. *Wi,* the god of the sun, provided warmth; from *Tate,* the wind, came the breath of life. *Ksa,* the god of wisdom, contributed intelligence. *Heyoka,* who had the power to destroy evil and nourish good and to promote abundance and growth, provided the power to produce offspring, and *Han*

Hepiwi, god of the moon, provided love and a longing for children.

She was captivated by everything Jacob told her. She had always loved Indians, had always been fascinated by their lifestyle and their customs and beliefs. She had read a lot in books and online but hearing it from Jacob made it more interesting, more real, more important.

When she wasn't cooking or cleaning or keeping Jacob company, she wrote on her current work in progress. More and more, the hero in her story took on the personality and physical characteristics of Cade Kills Thunder. More and more, she wished he would reconsider and pose for her cover.

On Wednesday, Jacob announced that he was feeling a little better and would be joining her and Cade for dinner. They were sitting at the dinner table that evening when Jacob suggested that Cade take Callie to a dance being held in town on Saturday night.

"It's an old-fashioned barn dance," Jacob said. "There will be fiddle playing and square dancing and apple cider." He grinned at the two of them. "You have both been working hard since you got back. You deserve a night off."

Callie glanced at Cade, then looked back at Jacob. "I don't think we should leave you…"

"Nothing to think about," Jacob said. "You have been cooped up with me long enough. It is time you went out and kicked up your heels. Isn't that right, grandson?"

Cade nodded. He knew his great-grandfather well, knew there was no point in arguing once the old man had made up his mind. With as much good grace as he could manage, he said, "Yes, *Tunkashila.*"

Jacob beamed at them. *"Waste yelo!"* Good!

Callie woke early the next morning. Rising, she opened the curtains and looked out the window. Nothing but blue sky and prairie as far as the eye could see. It was so beautiful here, so peaceful. At first, the quiet had bothered her. She was used to the sound of cars backfiring, sirens, the squeal of tires, dogs barking. Here, there was only the sound of cattle lowing, the whinny of a horse, birds calling to each other and occasionally the distant sound of a coyote. It was a pleasant change, one she was getting much too fond of.

After fixing breakfast for Cade and Jacob, she drove into town in search of a dress to wear to the dance. She didn't find a dress, but she did find a white off-the-shoulder blouse with a ruffled neckline and a calico skirt. She also bought a couple of fluffy petticoats and a pair of white boots that were fringed on the sides. Pleased with her purchases, she went to the grocery store and stocked up on the essentials—eggs, bread, bacon, steaks, beer and chocolate. To ease her conscience, she added fruit, vegetables, cheese and low-fat milk, as well as a couple boxes of cereal and anything else that caught her eye as she headed for the cash register.

The people in the store were very friendly, nodding when she passed them in the aisles. Several clerks asked if she was finding everything all right. The box boy loaded the bags into her trunk for her and wished her a nice day.

The drive back to the ranch was pleasant. There was little traffic. The sky was a blue so bright and clear it almost hurt her eyes to look at it. Cattle grazed on both sides of the road. She passed a herd of horses, a pasture filled with sheep. She saw goats and chickens and even a few pigs. And, high overhead, an eagle made long lazy circles as it drifted on the air currents.

It really was beautiful country, she thought, and knew she would miss the beauty of it when she returned to the city. She didn't even want to think about going home, which surprised her. She had always considered herself a city girl at heart.

"Maybe it's not the country you'll miss at all," she muttered as she turned onto the road that led to the ranch. "Maybe it's the country boy."

Said country boy was the first thing she saw when she pulled up in front of the house. He was climbing a ladder to the barn roof, a large box balanced on one broad shoulder. Shirtless, his long black hair gleaming black as a raven's wing in the sunlight, he was a sight to take her breath away.

Turning off the ignition, she opened the door and got out of the car, her gaze once again drawn to the roof of the barn and the man now kneeling there, fitting a shingle in place.

She purposefully took her time unloading the groceries from the trunk, unable to keep her gaze from straying to the man on the roof. The afternoon sunlight caressed his copper-hued skin. He wore a red bandana tied around his forehead to keep his hair out of his eyes. His jeans fit snugly over his tight buns. She licked her lips as she watched the muscles in his arms bunch and relax as he wielded the hammer with ease.

In the kitchen, she dropped the last sack on the table, then went to the window. Cade Kills Thunder was certainly a treat for the eyes, she thought, watching him nail a shingle in place. He moved with an unconscious grace that tightened the muscles in her stomach and made her mouth go dry. Made her long to run a finger down the vee in his back, to curl her hands around his biceps and feel the strength that resided there.

Turning away from the window, she put the groceries away, her movements accompanied by the steady rhythmic sound of hammering from outside.

She had just finished making lunch when the back door opened and Cade entered the kitchen, his shirt slung over one shoulder, bringing with him the smell of sunshine and sweat.

He nodded at her, then went to the sink to wash up. She watched him from the corner of her eye, her hands curled into fists to keep from reaching out to stroke his back, yearning to feel the heat of his skin beneath her palms.

Cade turned off the faucet and reached for a towel, fully aware of Callie's scrutiny. He'd thought the sun beating down on him outside was hot but it was nothing compared to the heat in the kitchen.

Tossing the towel aside, he shrugged into his shirt, then slowly turned to face her. A flush burned in her cheeks when she realized he had caught her staring at him.

What was there about her that she looked prettier every time he saw her? Even now, dressed in a pair of jeans and a short-sleeved sweater, her hair tied back in a ponytail, she looked good enough to eat. Hard to believe there had been a time when he didn't like red hair. Thick red hair that tempted his touch every time he saw it.

He watched her tuck a wayward lock behind her ear, wondering how she could turn such an ordinary gesture into something so sensual that it made his jeans feel two sizes too small.

He might have crossed the kitchen then and taken her in his arms. He might have kissed her. He might have dragged her out to the barn for a little old-fashioned necking. He might have done any or all of the things racing through his mind if Jacob hadn't chosen that moment to enter the kitchen.

"Jacob," Callie said, her voice a trifle shaky. "What are you doing out of bed?"

"Thought I might take my lunch in here today," he replied, making his way to the table and pulling out a chair. He sat down, his shrewd gaze moving from Cade's face to Callie's and back again. "How's the roof coming along?"

Cade sat down before his great-grandfather had time to notice his aroused state. "Another row and I'll be done."

Jacob nodded. "Good, good."

Callie set a plate in front of Jacob. "What would you like to drink?"

"Beer."

She glanced at Cade as she set his plate in front of him. "And you?"

"Beer sounds good to me, too."

She plucked two bottles from the fridge for the men, then poured herself a glass of lemonade and put the drinks on the table. Picking up her own plate, she took a chair between the two men.

Jacob took a bite of his sandwich, chewed a moment and then grinned. "We haven't eaten this good in…" He shook his head. "We've never eaten this good."

Callie smiled, pleased at his compliment. "It's nothing, really," she said, and indeed, it was nothing special—just tuna mixed with onions and pickles on sourdough bread, macaroni salad and potato chips. Hardly a gourmet meal.

She ate quietly, listening to Jacob and Cade discuss ranch business. She had a feeling that Cade knew she had been watching him when he was on the roof. She was tempted to tell him to keep his shirt on if he didn't want her staring at him, but she was afraid he might do just that.

She hated the wariness between them, missed the easy camaraderie they had shared on the drive to Jackson Hole. The sexual tension that had burned bright between them had drawn them even closer together, until he discovered that she wanted him to pose for the cover of her book. Even now, she didn't think he had believed her when she said she hadn't entered him in the cover-model contest. She didn't know who had. Kim, perhaps. It was the sort of thing Kim might do. Kim or Vicki or any one of the two hundred other women who had been at the conference.

Darn the man! Why did he have to be so stubborn? What would it hurt if he posed for the cover of one book? He'd never have to do it again if he didn't like it. But she didn't dare ask him again.

When lunch was over, Jacob went back to his room to take a nap and Cade went outside. Standing at the sink, doing the dishes, Callie watched Cade remove his shirt and climb the ladder to the roof once again.

Even if she hadn't been wildly attracted to him, even if she didn't like him more than she should, she would have been hard-pressed to turn away from the window. He made an imposing picture. She would have defied any woman under the age of ninety to look at Cade and not be moved.

Too restless to stay inside, she tossed the towel over the back of a chair, picked up her laptop and went outside.

Sitting down in the rocking chair on the porch, she lifted the lid on her laptop and called up her latest work in progress. But it wasn't her story that drew her attention. It was Cade Kills Thunder.

Hardly aware of the passing of time, she rocked slowly back and forth as she watched him work. She tried to figure out what it was about him that fascinated her so. She had seen handsome men before. Talked to them. Danced with them. Almost had an affair with one. What was there about this man that had captured her heart? And why did he have to be such a *stubborn* man? Well, she could be stubborn, too. It wouldn't hurt him to pose for her cover. Maybe his friends would rib him a little, but that was no big deal.

She tapped her finger on the arm of the rocker. One way or another, she was determined to have him on the cover of her next book. There had to be a way to convince him. Money was no incentive. Models didn't make that much, at least unknown ones. He wasn't interested in fame. What else could she offer him?

She immediately dismissed the obvious answer.

She closed her eyes, imagining him on the cover of her book. He'd be shirtless, of course, his long black hair blown by the wind. He'd hold a rifle cradled in his arm, or perhaps he'd be holding a feathered lance. She visualized a range of snowcapped mountains in the distance, or perhaps an Indian village stretched along a riverbank, or…he'd be astride a horse. Of course, that was it! He'd be riding a stallion as wild and untamed as the man. She smiled as the image took form in her mind.

"Hey, Red, what are you dreaming about?"

Her eyelids flew open at the sound of his voice. He was hunkered down beside the rocking chair, his shirt over one shoulder.

"Must have been a good dream, the way you were smiling," he remarked. "Was I in it?"

"Of course not!"

"No?" Raising up a little, he leaned forward and pressed his lips to hers.

A low moan of pleasure rose in her throat.

"Are you sure you weren't dreaming of me?" His lips brushed hers again. "Maybe I was kissing you here..." He kissed the sensitive spot behind her ear. "Or here..." His lips moved up and down her neck, eliciting shivers of delight, then returned to her mouth. His hand cupped the back of her head and he drew her closer, deepening the kiss.

All thought fled her mind as he drew her into his lap. She wrapped her arms around him, surrendering to his embrace, reveling in the touch of his hands gliding over her back. Somehow, they were lying on the porch, his body poised over hers, his tongue stroking her lips.

She stared up at him, breathless. "What are you doing?"

"I'm learning to find my way," he replied, dropping a kiss on the tip of her nose. "I never go anywhere without mapping the route." His hand moved slowly over her thigh. "I need to know the terrain." His hand slid up over her hip. "Which is the best road to take." His hand skimmed her breast ever so lightly. "Whether there are mountains. Or valleys."

He was kissing her again, his body draped intimately over hers, when she let out a yelp.

With a start, Cade raised up on his elbows, his brow furrowed as he stared down at her through dark hungry eyes.

She shifted beneath him, breathless and a little embarrassed. "Something's poking me."

One dark eyebrow rose.

"Not you," she said, her cheeks flaming.

Rising, he offered her his hand and pulled her to her feet.

Callie reached around behind her and withdrew the large splinter that had been stabbing her in the back. There was blood on the end.

Cade frowned as he took it from her hand. "Come on, we'd better get some antiseptic on that."

Taking her by the hand, he led her upstairs to the bathroom where he washed the affected area, then applied an antiseptic salve and a bandage.

"Better?" he asked.

"Yes, thank you."

His gaze moved over her, still hot and hungry. "We could resume what we were doing in a more comfortable place," he suggested.

It was tempting, so very very tempting.

"Red?"

"No, I can't. I…I've got to get some work done. I…I've got a deadline, and…"

He held up in hands in surrender. "All right, all right," he said with a wry grin. "I wouldn't want to keep you from turning out the next bestseller."

With a nod, she fled the room, thinking that curling up with her laptop would be a poor replacement for being wrapped in the arms of Cade Kills Thunder.

Chapter Thirteen

It was difficult to face Cade over dinner that night. Every time he looked her way, she remembered what had happened on the porch earlier, couldn't help wondering how much further things might have gone between them if that darn splinter hadn't jabbed her in the back. Of course, they would have had to stop before they went all the way. After all, they had been *outside,* for goodness' sakes!

"So," Cade said, sitting back in his chair. "Did you get a lot of writing done this afternoon?"

She stared at him, wondering what would serve her best, the truth or a little white lie. The truth was, she had spent a good deal of the afternoon thinking about Cade and what had almost happened between them, and then she had written a love scene that was so hot she was surprised her laptop hadn't gone up in flames.

"Red?"

"I didn't get a lot written," she said, deciding on the truth, "but what I wrote was really good."

"I'd like to read it," Jacob said, smiling.

"Oh." She searched her mind for a good excuse, thinking she would rather die than let Jacob read that love scene. "I...that is, well, I hope you understand, but I never let anyone read my works in progress."

He looked disappointed, but nodded.

"Why is that?" Cade asked.

"Just a superstition of mine."

"I see."

Callie picked at the food left on her plate, afraid that he saw way too much.

When dinner was over, the men went into the living room, leaving Callie to clean up the kitchen and do the dishes. She was grateful for the time alone. When she was finished, she bid the men good-night, using her writing as an excuse to go up to her room early.

She spent the night dreaming of him, and in that dream, they finished what they had started on the porch.

She woke in the morning feeling guilty for that dream. It had been so vivid and seemed so real, she wouldn't have been surprised to find him lying next to her looking satisfied and pleased with himself.

Rising, she took a quick shower, then dressed and went downstairs to fix breakfast. She was fixing French toast and bacon when Cade entered the kitchen.

"Something smells good," he remarked, coming up behind her.

A shiver ran down her spine at his nearness. "Probably the bacon."

"It's not bacon, Red," he drawled. "It's you."

She moaned softly as he nuzzled the back of her neck. If she could bottle whatever it was he had, she could make millions.

"So," he asked, "what are you doing after breakfast?"

She swallowed hard. "What did you have in mind?"

He chuckled. "Not what I'd like. Jacob wants me to exercise his horse. I thought maybe you'd like to go riding with me."

"I don't know how to ride."

"Don't worry, darlin', I can teach you."

The way he said "darlin'" sent yet another shiver down her spine, making her wonder if they were still talking about horseback riding.

An hour later, she was standing in front of the barn, having second thoughts as she watched Cade saddle his horse. She would have been happy to stand there all day, just watching him. Leaning against the barn door, she admired the way he moved, the way the muscles rippled beneath his shirt, the easy way he handled the horses. He picked the dirt from the gelding's hooves, brushed the animal's coat with quick efficient strokes, smoothed the blanket in place, lifted the heavy saddle as if it weighed four pounds instead of forty. He cinched the saddle in place and then moved to the second horse, a pretty little brown mare that was slightly swaybacked.

Callie had always loved horses. They were such beautiful creatures, but, unlike most of the friends she'd had when she was young, she had never had much of a desire to own a horse, much less ride one. They were such big creatures and even though these two looked docile enough, she had seen enough movies and done enough research to know that horses were capable of bucking wildly and, on occasion, running away with their riders. While her friends had been out taking riding lessons, she had preferred to stay home, curled up with a book.

Cade cinched the saddle on the second horse, dropped the reins over the animal's neck, and turned to Callie. "Ready?"

She nodded warily.

"This here's Misty. She's old and settled, perfect for a greenhorn."

Callie moved up beside the horse and gave her a tentative pat on the neck. The mare blew softly, then rubbed her forehead against Callie's chest. Callie looked up at Cade. "Does that mean she likes me?"

"Sure 'nough." Putting his hands around her waist, Cade lifted her into the saddle, adjusted the stirrups, and handed her the reins.

When he was sure she was comfortable, he swung onto the back of Jacob's horse. "Don't worry, we'll take it nice and slow."

Clucking to his mount, Cade led the way out of the yard.

Misty followed without any urging from Callie, who clung to the reins and the saddle horn as the mare moved out.

"Just relax," Cade advised, glancing over his shoulder.

"Easy for you to say," Callie muttered. However, as they followed a narrow path through a stand of timber, she stopped worrying about falling off. Misty had a smooth, even gait and Callie found herself admiring the view—not the trees and the flora and fauna, but the broad expanse of Cade's back, the easy way he sat in his saddle.

Callie uttered a little gasp of pleasure as the path widened into a broad meadow bordered by tall trees. A shallow stream ran through the center of the meadow. Wildflowers grew in scattered clumps, making bright splashes of color against the brilliant green of the grass.

Cade pulled up, waiting for Callie to join him. "How are you doing?"

"Fine." She patted Misty on the neck. "I never thought I'd enjoy riding, but it's wonderful."

He smiled, pleased by the excitement in her voice, the glow in her eyes.

"Can I ask you something?"

He shrugged. "Sure."

"Do you believe that rocks are alive, that they have a spirit?"

Cade stared at her, then grinned. "You've been talking to Jacob, haven't you?"

"Yes."

"Did he tell you any Coyote stories?"

"A couple… So, do you believe the rocks are alive?"

"'Fraid so." He regarded her from beneath his hat brim for a few minutes. "What do you believe?"

"The usual things, I guess, but I kind of like the idea of believing that everything has its own spirit. I don't know about rocks and mountains being alive…" She paused, frowning. "But then, I believe the earth is alive, so I guess it's not much of a stretch to believe the mountains and the rocks are alive, too."

"We'll make an Indian out of you yet."

"I'd like that."

They rode in silence for another mile or so, and then Cade drew his horse to a halt. "I don't want you to overdo it the first time," he said. "I need to let Jester run a bit. Why don't you wait here while I let him run, and then we'll ride around the meadow before we head back?"

"All right."

Cade touched a heel to his horse's flanks and the big gelding moved out at a brisk trot that quickly stretched into a canter.

Callie pressed a hand to her heart as the gelding bucked a few times, then settled down into an easy lope. What a picture they made, man and horse, as they galloped around the edge of the meadow. She wished now that she had taken those riding lessons years ago.

A quarter of an hour later, Cade rode up beside her, grinning with pleasure.

"Was he supposed to buck like that?" Callie asked.

"Shoot, that wasn't a buck," Cade said, slapping the gelding on the neck. "He was just feeling good."

"Oh."

"Come on," Cade said, "let's see how you do at a trot."

At first, she bounced around like a kernel of popcorn in a popper but, with Cade's instruction, she soon learned to sit deep in the saddle, to synchronize her movements with those of the horse.

"Better," Cade said. He slowed his horse to a walk, then drew rein under a tree.

She smiled at him, thinking how much she liked being with him, how good he made her feel.

With a gentle tug on the reins, Cade eased his horse up close to Callie's, so that they were facing each other, their knees and thighs touching. "I'll make a horsewoman out of you yet."

"I thought you were going to make an Indian of me."

"That, too."

Their gazes met and held and then, ever so slowly, Cade leaned toward her, one hand sliding around her waist, drawing her toward him. Her heart skipped a beat as his mouth closed on hers. His mouth was warm and firm. Heat spread through her, speared its way to the pit of her stomach.

His horse stirred and stamped its foot, breaking the contact between them. "You're a quick study, Red," Cade remarked.

His voice moved over her, husky with yearning. She thought he might kiss her again, was keenly disappointed when he settled back into the saddle. "You ready to go back?"

She nodded, wishing he would kiss her again, grateful that he didn't. Another kiss like that and she would be begging him to make love to her right there in the tall grass.

When they returned to the barn, he sent her up to the house to look in on Jacob while he unsaddled the horses. Callie wanted to stay with Cade but it seemed wiser to put some distance between them, at least for a little while.

She was smiling when she reached the house. Tomorrow night, at the dance, she would have the perfect excuse to be in his arms.

Chapter Fourteen

The next afternoon while fixing lunch, all Callie could think about was Cade. She hadn't seen much of him after she returned to the house yesterday. She had spent most of the rest of the day with Jacob, listening as the old man reminisced about growing up on the reservation. He had told her about his great-great-grandfather who had lived in the shining times before the white man invaded the land of the Lakota.

Now, sitting at the kitchen table across from him, she listened as he continued to reminisce about the past.

"Those were the good days," Jacob said. "The best days, when the Lakota people lived wild and free and our only enemies were the Crow. Those were the days when our brother, the buffalo, roamed the prairie. The hunting was always good then. The People had hides for their lodges and plenty of hump meat and tongue. In those days, our brother, the eagle, carried the prayers of the People to *Wakan Tanka*, the Great Spirit."

"It must have been a good life."

Jacob paused, his thoughts obviously turned to the past.

Callie had done a lot of research on Indians and the Old West and she knew quite a bit about how the Indians had lived. Jacob might have thought of it as a good life, and perhaps it had been, but she couldn't imagine living that way—cooking over an open fire, skinning animals for their hides, tanning those hides for clothing. No dentists, no doctors to help with childbirth, and yet the Indian women had done it and survived. She knew that many of the herbs and plants that the Indian shamans had used for healing were still used today.

"And then," Jacob said heavily, "the *wasichu* came and our life was never the same again."

Callie nodded. She had always felt a deep regret at the fate of the Indians and yet, the strong had always preyed upon the weak. She had read somewhere, though she wasn't sure how true it was, that one of the reasons the Indians had lost their battles to the whites was that they did not understand the white man's way of fighting. The Indians fought for horses and glory and the counting of coup and when they felt they had fought enough or won glory enough, they went home. The white man did not fight like that. He fought to win. He fought to the death.

She remembered reading about the Battle of the Little Big Horn and how, after the Indians had killed Custer and his men, they went out again the next day to fight the soldiers who had dug in on another hill and how, after a brief battle, Sitting Bull had told his warriors that they had fought enough, killed enough and left the valley of the Greasy Grass.

She said as much to Jacob, who nodded. "My great-great-grandfather was there that day. He said it was a fight that would never be forgotten. He was a man who hated the *wasichu* but he said most of them fought bravely that day."

She could see it clearly in her mind's eye as Jacob told her what had been told to him so many years ago—the soldiers, badly outnumbered, gathered together on what was now known as Custer Hill. They must have known they were fighting a battle they couldn't win. Did they curse Custer for not listening to his scouts, for refusing to believe there were thousands of Indians gathered in the valley? She could only imagine their fear as the Indians rode toward them, thousands of mounted Lakota and Arapaho and Cheyenne, Indians determined to avenge the deaths of their loved ones and the wrongs that had been done to them on the reservations.

She imagined Crazy Horse riding at the head of his warriors, but in her mind's eye, the figure racing over the plains astride a spotted pony was that of Cade Kills Thunder.

Later, while Jacob took a nap, she went outside and walked around the ranch yard. She told herself she just wanted a little fresh air, but she knew she was only kidding herself. She was hoping to see Cade.

Wandering down to the barn, she looked inside, noticing then that his horse was gone. No doubt Cade was out riding the range, cowboy-style.

She took a few minutes to pet one of the other horses, then went outside. Clyde looked up as she neared his corral and she stopped to look at him, a little apprehensive when he lumbered toward her.

"He's a pet," she reminded herself as he drew closer. When he lowered his head, she bit down on her lower lip, then reached out and scratched between his horns. His hair was remarkably soft, his head as hard as a rock.

It must have been exciting, if somewhat dangerous, hunting the buffalo, chasing them across the grassy plains. She could almost hear the thunder of their hooves, the cries of the warriors as they rode in pursuit, the hiss of arrows. Later, the women would have come out of hiding to skin the huge beasts and cut up the meat. She remembered the scene in *Dances With Wolves* when Wind in His Hair had cut open the buffalo and offered the heart to Lieutenant Dunbar. Back in 1991, she and Hilda had gone to a lecture at a local museum and been fortunate enough to meet Neil Travis, one of the men who had worked on the production. During the course of the evening, he had shown a short movie about the making of the film. Travis won an Academy Award for editing the film. He had brought his Oscar with him, and after the lecture, he had let Callie hold it. She had been surprised at how heavy it was. Ever since then, it had been her dream to win one, perhaps for best screenplay. Though she couldn't swear to it now, it had been so long ago, she seemed to recall being told that the "heart" Kevin Costner had taken a bite out of had been made of gelatin. She grinned, remembering that the buffalo they had used in one of the scenes had also been named Clyde. In order to make Clyde run toward the young Indian boy left standing when his horse ran away, someone had stood behind the boy holding up cookies, which the buffalo apparently had a fondness for.

In the old days, the Plains Indians had called the buffalo their brother and when they killed one, they always thanked the animal for giving up its life so that the People might live, and left behind a bit of meat. The buffalo had not only provided the Indians with meat, but with hides for clothing and blankets and lodge covers. Their horns had been used for spoons, their tails as fly whisks, their hair for thread. Glue had been made from their hooves, waterskins from their intestines. It was no wonder the Lakota felt such rage when the whites came and slaughtered the buffalo, taking only the tongues and the hides and leaving thousands of pounds of meat to rot in the sun.

She scratched Clyde's head again, glad that white hunters and settlers had not hunted the buffalo to extinction.

Turning away from the corral, she went up to the house to fix Jacob's lunch. But it wasn't Jacob she was thinking about—it was Cade and the kiss they had shared the day before, and the dance in town later that night.

She ran a hand through her hair, suddenly nervous at the

thought of meeting people he knew. She hadn't asked what people wore to these shindigs. Maybe her skirt and blouse were too casual, or too dressy.

Well, there was no point in worrying about it now. She didn't have time to go looking for anything else.

She was glad when it was time to fix dinner. She needed something to think about, something besides meeting Cade's friends.

Jacob wandered into the kitchen a short time later and a few minutes after that, Cade came in the back door.

Callie said little during dinner, content to listen while the two men talked about the price of feed and water holes and whether they should breed one of their mares to Jed Henry's studhorse.

When dinner was over, Jacob went outside to feed Kola.

Cade pushed away from the table and dropped his napkin beside his plate. "You're a good cook," he remarked.

"Thank you."

He cleared his throat. "We should leave about seven."

"I'll be ready."

He stood there, looking across the table at her. Heat flowed between them, an electric awareness so hot he wouldn't have been surprised to see flames shimmering in the air between them.

Did she feel it? How could she not? He turned away before she could see the effect she was having on him. "See ya later," he muttered, and left the room.

Chapter Fifteen

Cade stared into the mirror as he wiped the last of the lather from his face. He didn't know whether he wanted to strangle his great-grandfather for pushing him into taking Callie to the dance, or buy the old man that big-screen TV he'd been wanting. Truth be told, Cade had been looking forward to spending the evening with Callie ever since Jacob mentioned it, something that had been intensified by the ride they had taken together yesterday and the heat that had flowed between them in the kitchen earlier. He had to admit he enjoyed her company, and even though he had been angry when he found out what she'd been up to at the conference, he couldn't stop thinking about her, or remembering how well her body fit his, or how sweet her lips had been. Couldn't stop dreaming about her at night. He grunted softly. The last time he'd had such lusty dreams, he'd been sixteen and as randy as an old goat.

He rinsed the soap from his razor, ran a hand over his jaw, tossed the towel wrapped around his middle into the clothes hamper and then padded into his bedroom to get dressed. It had been a long time since he had taken a date to a town dance. Once his buddies got a good look at Callie, he'd probably have to fight them off with a stick.

When he was dressed, he sat on the edge of the bed to pull on his socks and boots, then grabbed his hat and headed downstairs. He didn't know what there was about Callie, but she had him feeling like a teenager calling on a girl for the first time.

She was waiting for him in the living room. A tentative smile curved her lips when he entered the room.

Cade's heart skipped a beat. Damn, she looked as pretty as a little red filly in a field of prairie flowers. The ruffled, off-the-shoulder blouse she wore was feminine and alluring, the full skirt swished when she walked.

"Evenin'."

She smiled at him, obviously pleased by the admiration she'd seen in his eyes. "Hi."

"Are you ready to go?"

"Yes."

"You'd best bring a jacket. The hall's pretty drafty."

"I've got one."

He grunted softly as she picked up the long black coat draped over the back of the sofa. He might have noticed it earlier if he hadn't been so busy looking at the woman. "Let's go, then."

With a nod, she walked toward the door.

He held it open for her, then followed her outside. Her perfume tickled his nostrils.

"Do you want to take my car?" she asked.

"Sure, if you don't mind."

Reaching into her handbag, she pulled out her keys. Her fingertips brushed against his as she handed him the key ring.

With a little gasp, she stared up at him, then quickly looked away.

He blew out a deep breath as he held the door open for her. It was going to be a long night.

They spoke little on the way into town. Callie gazed out the window, pretending to watch the scenery, all too aware of the man sitting so close beside her. His presence, the sheer size of the man, made the car seem smaller than it was.

"Do you think Jacob will be up and around soon?" she asked at length.

"I hope so. I suppose you're anxious to get back home."

"Oh, no," she said quickly, then bit down on her lower lip.

Cade slid a glance in her direction. "You're welcome to stay here as long as you want."

"Thank you," she said, wondering if he would think forever was too long.

The dance was in full swing when they arrived. It was exactly like Callie had imagined dances would be in the Old West. There was red, white and blue bunting draped along the walls. Snowy linen cloths covered tables laden with cakes, cookies, pies, muffins and scones. Tin washtubs held cans of soda, bottles and cans of beer, and bottled water. A makeshift stage was set up in one corner. A three-piece band provided music, while a tall man wearing a gaudy red-and-gold shirt and a huge white hat called a square dance.

Taking her hand, Cade led her around the edge of the dance floor. Following his lead, she hung her jacket on a wooden peg.

Callie noticed that several women smiled at him. One brushed up against him, a predatory look in her eyes.

"Hey, sweet stuff, when did you get home?" the woman asked, her voice a husky purr.

"A while ago. How you doing, Gracie?"

"Why don't you come over some night and see for yourself?" she asked, bold as brass.

Cade laughed. "Go on, behave yourself now."

Gracie winked at him. "What fun would that be?" With a flick of her full skirt, she turned and walked away.

"An old friend?" Callie asked, hoping she didn't sound as jealous as she felt.

"You could say that," Cade replied.

"I guess you have a lot of 'old friends.'"

A grin twitched at the corner of his mouth. "One or two."

She thought ten or twenty would be more like it but didn't say so. As the evening wore on, she thought her estimate was way too low. It seemed every woman in the place knew Cade though, thankfully, few were as blatant as Gracie.

"Certainly no shortage of cows tonight," Callie muttered as yet another woman headed their way to stop and say hello to Cade.

He laughed out loud, then tweaked her nose. "Come on, Red, I'm thirsty, let's go get something to drink."

She followed him around the room to where the drinks were.

"What do you want? Beer or soda?"

"Anything but milk," she muttered under her breath.

"What?"

"Soda."

She watched him delve into the tub that held the sodas. He pulled out a green can and handed it to her, then popped the top on a beer can and took a long swallow.

There was a round of applause as the set ended.

"Would you like to dance?" Cade asked.

She glanced at the couples on the floor. "I don't know how to square-dance."

"Come on, there's a square forming. Just follow the other ladies."

"All right."

Cade took the can from her hand and set it on a table alongside his, then took her arm and led her onto the floor. Just before the music started, he informed her that they were a side couple.

A few moments later, she was in the midst of her first square dance. Just "following the other ladies" was a bit more complicated than it sounded. Fortunately, the other dancers were willing to put up with her mistakes as she stumbled her way through "forward and back," "star promenade," "alle-mande left," "right and left grand," and "all four ladies chain."

Cade was light on his feet and even though she felt like the proverbial bull in a china shop, he made her feel light on her feet, too, especially when he took her in his arms and swung her around. Once she started to get the hang of it, Callie had to admit it was a lot of fun. She didn't know if it was the danc-ing or being in Cade's arms that left her breathless, but after two sets, she was ready for a break and another soda. She'd always thought square dancing was for old fogies but she soon changed her mind. A body had to be mighty spry to keep up with the caller and she resolved then and there to get into some kind of exercise program as soon as she got back to Los Angeles.

Cade found an empty table outside and left her there while he went back inside to get them something to eat.

Callie sat back in her chair, enjoying the beauty of the night. The sky was adorned with a million twinkling stars. A full moon smiled down on them. The air was filled with the sound of crickets and music and laughter.

Her heart skipped a beat when she saw Cade walking to-ward her. Clad in a dark blue Western shirt, new jeans and black boots, he was the sexiest thing she had ever seen.

He handed her a slice of chocolate cake and a paper cup filled with lemonade. "Hope that's all right."

"Chocolate is always all right." She took a bite and sighed with pleasure. Whoever baked the cake was a chocolate lover, too, she thought. The frosting was fudge, sinfully thick and rich.

Cade sat down across from her and dug into a huge piece of apple pie. He looked up at her and grinned around a mouth-ful. "Can't beat Emma Underhill's apple pie." He dug into it again, then held his fork out to her. "Want a bite?"

The thought of eating from his fork was more tempting than the pie.

Cade felt a sudden tightness in his groin as Callie leaned forward to accept his offering. He couldn't take his gaze from her mouth as it closed over the fork. Right then, he would have given half the ranch to be that piece of pie. And when she licked her lips…damn! He had it bad and it was getting worse.

Conscious of his regard, Callie wiped her mouth with her napkin, wondering if the night had suddenly grown warmer. Reaching for her cup, she took a long drink, hoping it would cool her off and ease the butterflies in her stomach.

"Ready to go back in?" Cade asked.

"Are you sure they won't mind putting up with me again?"

"I'm sure. Come on. They were all beginners at one time, you know."

Back inside, they discovered that the caller and the band had taken a break.

"I guess we're out of luck," Callie was saying when, suddenly, music filled the air.

"Jukebox," Cade explained, and taking her by the hand, he led her onto the dance floor.

The tune was an oldie that had once been known as a make-out song. Cade drew her into his arms and she rested her head on his chest, eyes closed, while they danced. Everything else seemed to fade away until all she was aware of was Cade's arm around her waist, his hand holding hers, the crisp cotton of his shirt beneath her cheek, the warmth of his body against hers.

They moved together effortlessly, as if they had danced together countless times before.

Cade drew Callie a little closer, every fiber of his being aware of the woman in his arms. He hadn't been so easily aroused since he was a randy teenager, yet all he had to do was look at Callie and his hormones went into overdrive. Every breath he took carried the fragrance of her perfume, the floral scent of soap and shampoo. And woman. Unable to resist, he lowered his head and nuzzled her hair, loving the silky feel of it against his cheek. Closing his eyes for a moment, he had a quick image of the two of them in his bed, arms and legs in an intimate tangle, her hair brushing his chest.

He opened his eyes as heat surged through him, glanced down at Callie to see if she was aware of his aroused state. Judging by the faint blush in her cheeks, he assumed she was.

He put a little distance between them, hoping the music didn't end right away.

He was leading her off the dance floor a few moments later when three of his neighbors came striding toward them.

Cade groaned softly. It wasn't that he didn't like Norton, Housley and Dockstader; it was just that he wanted to be alone with Callie.

"Hey, Big Thunder!" Norton said, slapping him on the back. "Long time no see!"

"How are you doing, Frank?" Cade asked.

"Fine, just fine." Frank Norton's gaze moved over Callie. "I don't have to ask how you're doing."

"Callie, this is Frank Norton," Cade said, slipping his arm around her waist in a decidedly male gesture of possession. "And these two characters are Whip Housley and Curly Dockstader."

"Good evening, gentlemen," Callie said, nodding at each one in turn.

Curly Dockstader was a short, stocky man with close-cropped brown hair and squinty brown eyes. Whip Housley was tall and reed thin, with a shock of wheat-blond hair and gray eyes. Frank Norton could best be described as average—average height, average weight, light brown hair and blue eyes.

"You're the writer, aren't you?" Dockstader asked.

Cade frowned, wondering how Dockstader knew who she was.

"Yes, I am," Callie replied.

Dockstader elbowed Norton in the ribs. "Told ya so."

Norton nodded. "You're a lot prettier than your picture, ma'am."

"Which picture is that?" Callie asked.

Dockstader reached into his shirt pocket and pulled out a piece of paper. He unfolded it carefully and offered it to Callie.

Cade glanced at the photo. It showed Callie accepting her award at the conference.

"Personally," Norton said, grinning broadly, "I like the other one better."

"What other one?"

"This one," Dockstader said. With a flourish, he reached into his shirt pocket again and withdrew a second piece of paper.

Cade groaned inwardly as he stared at the grainy black-and-white image. It was another photo taken at the conference, but this one wasn't of Callie. It was a picture of Cade, taken during the cover-model contest. And it wasn't just any photo, but one of him without his shirt.

"So, Cade," Norton said, "when are we gonna see you on the cover of one of those bodice rippers?"

"Can we come watch?" Housley asked with a leer.

"Yeah, I've seen some of those covers," Dockstader said. "I'd love to see one of those female models up close."

"Well, don't hold your breath," Cade said, "'cause I'm not doing it."

"Man, I'd do it, just for a chance to hold one of those luscious models," Housley said.

"Talk to Callie, here. Maybe she'll put in a good word for you with her editor."

"Yeah," Dockstader said, laughing. "I'll bet they get a lot of calls for toothpicks."

Housley glared at Norton. "About as many as they get for midgets, I reckon."

Cade shook his head. "I'll talk to you guys later," he said and taking Callie by the hand, he led her out of the building.

"I guess we're leaving," she said as he practically dragged her toward her car.

"You guessed right."

They were heading for the parking lot when someone called Cade's name.

Cade didn't stop, didn't pay any attention to the man weaving his way toward them. Luther Pendleton was a troublemaker and always had been.

"Hey, Injun, I'm talkin' to ya."

"Go home and sleep it off, Luther."

"You think I'm drunk?" the man asked, his tone implying that the mere idea was an insult.

"I've never seen you any other way."

Luther stepped in front of Cade and jabbed a finger in his chest. "Always thinkin' you're better than anybody else! Hah! I seen that picture of you in the paper. Struttin' around like you was somebody special when you're nothing but a dirty half-breed bas…"

It happened so quickly, Callie almost missed it. One minute, Luther was hurling insults; the next, he was flat on his back on the ground, with blood trickling from his nose.

Cade took Callie by the arm and practically carried her to the car.

He unlocked the door, opened it for her and closed it with a bang before going around to the driver's side.

Callie bit down on her lip as he slid behind the wheel, wondering if it was a good idea for him to be driving in his current state of mind. She braced herself, expecting him to gun the engine and tear out onto the road. But it didn't happen. Cade started the engine and eased out of the parking space, stopped at the driveway and looked both ways before pulling into the street.

She chided herself for worrying. Cade wasn't a teenager. He was a grown man, one who drove a big rig for a living. He wasn't foolish enough to take his anger out behind the wheel.

Relaxing, Callie cast about for something to say to ease the tense silence between them but nothing came to mind.

Darn Luther and those other guys! Between the four of them, they had ruined what had been a perfectly lovely evening.

Cade pulled up in front of the house and killed the engine. Callie didn't wait for him to get out of the car and open the door for her. She couldn't stand to be in the close confines of the car with him for one more minute.

Muttering, "Good night," she opened the door and practically ran up the porch steps and didn't stop until she was safely in her room with the door locked.

Once inside, she paced the floor, shrugging out of her clothes as she did so. Her blouse landed on the dresser; her new skirt was a splash of color on the floor; one shoe skittered under the bed, the other ended up on top of her skirt.

Men! If she lived to be a hundred, she would never understand any of them.

Pulling on her nightgown and robe, she went down the hall to the bathroom to brush her teeth.

Back in her room again, she sat down on the edge of the bed. Staring at the rug on the floor, she recalled how wonderful it had been to dance with Cade. She had basked in his nearness, reveled in the feel of his arms around her. Of all the rotten luck! Who would have thought that photos from a conference in Jackson Hole would make their way here? If it hadn't been for Dockstader, Norton, and Housley she might still be at the dance with Cade, enjoying the music and each other's company.

And then she remembered Luther. Cade had hit the man with the speed of a striking snake. Even now, she didn't remember seeing Cade move. One minute he had been standing beside her, his jaw set, his eyes as cold as chips of black ice while Luther flung insults at him. The next minute, Luther had been out cold on the ground. She had to wonder who Luther the loudmouth was and why there was such animosity between Luther and Cade.

With a sigh, she went to the window to close the curtains. It was then that she saw Cade. He was riding a big buckskin horse bareback in the corral below her window. Shirtless and barefooted, with the moonlight shining down on him, he looked wild and carefree and oh so sexy.

He rode effortlessly, the reins held loosely in one hand, his other hand resting on his thigh.

After a time, he wheeled the horse around and rode in the other direction and then he put the horse through a series of quick moves that the horse executed flawlessly, at least as far as she could tell.

It was beautiful to watch, a midnight ballet on horseback, as man and animal moved together as one. The buckskin turned right and left and backed up, apparently on cue, though Callie never saw Cade signal the horse in any way.

She lost track of time as she stood there, watching, mesmerized by the speed and power of the horse, the unconscious sensuality of the man. She yearned to run downstairs, to climb up behind Cade, to wrap her arms around his waist, to rest her head on his bare back and feel the warmth of his skin against her cheek.

Heat flowed through her veins as she imagined herself surrendering to her heart's desire and running outside. Would he be pleased to see her? They had shared some truly amazing kisses, yet little had been said between them. The attraction between them was potent, yet they had not really spoken of it. He had never asked her to stay. If it weren't for Jacob, she would be back home now, rattling around her condo, yearning to be with Cade.

Biting down on her lower lip, she stared at the man below. Maybe it was time one of them said something. If he rebuffed her, she could always leave in the morning. And if he didn't…her heart skipped a beat and a warm flush spread up her neck into her cheeks.

If he didn't, she might find herself living in Montana.

Chapter Sixteen

Callie left the room, her heart pounding with excitement and trepidation. If he rejected her, or, worse yet, laughed at her, she would probably never get over it, but it was a chance she was willing to take. She practically ran down the stairs, afraid that if she stopped and thought about what she was about to do, her courage might desert her.

She was about to open the front door when she heard a loud crash. With a start, she glanced over her shoulder. The noise had come from Jacob's room.

Hurrying down the hall, she opened the door to the old man's room and flicked on the light switch, murmured, "Oh, my!" when she saw him sprawled facedown on the floor.

"Jacob!" Hurrying to his side, she knelt beside him and gently turned him over. A bruise was already forming on his brow. His breathing was labored and shallow. "Jacob! Oh, Lord, Jacob!"

Pulling a blanket off the bed, she spread it over him, then ran outside. She hurried toward the corral, only to find it empty.

"Cade! Cade, where are you?"

"What are you yelling about?" he asked, coming out of the barn.

"It's Jacob. He…"

But Cade wasn't listening. He was already running toward the house.

Callie ran after him, a silent prayer in her heart as she followed him into Jacob's room. She stood in the doorway, one hand pressed to her heart, while Cade examined the old man. Wrapping Jacob in the blanket, Cade stood.

"Call the hospital and tell them I'm on my way," he said. He didn't wait for an answer, just swept past her, the old man cradled like a child in his arms.

Callie quickly went to the phone and called information, then called the hospital and told them Cade would be arriving with his great-grandfather.

When that was done, she went into the kitchen and fixed herself a cup of coffee. After that, there was nothing to do but pace the floor, which only made her more nervous.

Going upstairs, she threw off her robe and gown, shrugged into a sweater and a pair of jeans and pulled on a pair of boots. Downstairs, she called the hospital for directions, then grabbed her keys and left the house.

Heedless of the speed limit, she put the pedal to the metal, grateful that there was no one on the road at this hour of the night.

She roared into the parking lot and turned into the first vacant space. Switching off the engine, she exited the car and ran toward the emergency entrance.

She found Cade sitting in one of the waiting rooms, a cup of coffee cradled in his hands.

He looked up as she entered the room.

"Have you heard anything?" Callie asked, dropping into the hard plastic chair beside his.

Cade shook his head. "Could be a stroke. Could be a heart attack. All they know for sure right now is that he's got a slight concussion from hitting his head when he fell."

"I'm sure he'll be all right," Callie said, though she wasn't sure at all.

Cade nodded. "Yeah."

He didn't sound any more convinced than she did.

Callie glanced around the room. A large round clock showed that it was a little after midnight. The television, situated on a corner shelf, was turned to a late night movie, the sound turned so low as to be inaudible. She hated hospitals, hated the antiseptic smell, the icky green walls, the ugly linoleum. She knew it was only her imagination, but every time she was in a hospital, she imagined she could see death lurking in every shadow, waiting.

She took a deep breath. Sometimes a vivid imagination was not a good thing.

"I'm gonna get another cup of coffee," Cade said, rising. "Do you want anything?"

"Coffee's fine, thanks."

With a nod, he left the room. Callie glanced at the television again. The movie, *Rachel and the Stranger,* was an old one, but it was one of her favorites.

Cade returned a few minutes later carrying two polystyrene cups. Sitting down, he handed her one.

She murmured her thanks.

He grunted softly.

After what seemed like an eternity but was probably no more than an hour, the doctor stepped into the room.

Cade rose immediately. "How is he?"

"Resting comfortably. He had a mild heart attack, so we'll want to keep an eye on him for a couple of days."

"Can I see him?"

"If you like."

Cade offered his hand to the doctor. "Thanks."

The doctor smiled as he shook Cade's hand. "Don't worry. He'll be home in a few days."

Callie breathed a sigh of relief. Turning to look at Cade, she was surprised to see tears in his eyes. Going to him, she put her arms around his waist.

"Are you all right?"

"Sure." His voice was gruff.

"You heard the doctor. He's going to be fine."

"Yeah." He took a deep breath, then rested his chin on the top of her head. He held her for a long time, saying nothing.

She was content to hold him. Seeing his tears made her ache inside.

"Why don't you go back to the ranch," he said after awhile. "I'm gonna stay here tonight."

"All right, if that's what you want."

He looked down at her. "What do you mean?"

"Just that I'll stay and keep you company, if you like."

His gaze moved over her and even though the timing was all wrong, she yearned for him to say the words she longed to hear.

Instead, he gave her a squeeze, then let her go. "No sense both of us spending the night on those uncomfortable chairs. Anyway, I could use you at home to look after the stock. Think you could do that for me?"

"I think so."

"Just drop some hay to the horses and throw some feed out for the chickens."

"All right. You'll call me if anything…you'll call me?"

"Yeah." He ran a hand through his hair. "I need to call my folks, too."

"Well, I guess I'll go."

His gaze moved over her again. "Thanks, Red."

Just two words, but they warmed her through and through.

Smiling, she left the hospital. She was still smiling when she climbed into bed.

* * *

She slept late the following morning and then jumped out of bed, certain that Cade would have had the animals fed and watered by now.

Dressing quickly, she hurried down to the barn, climbed the ladder to the loft and dropped hay to the horses. She found chicken feed in a big barrel. Scooping some into a bucket, she carried it outside and scattered it around, yelping when a rooster came too close for comfort.

She threw a flake of hay to Clyde and then draped her arms over the top rail of the corral, watching the buffalo eat.

Returning to the house, she took a moment to scratch Kola's ears, then plugged in her laptop and tried to get some writing done on her current work in progress, but for once she couldn't lose herself in her characters, couldn't think of anything but Cade and Jacob.

Needing something to do, she called home and checked her messages. There was a message from her mother, informing her that they were having the annual family reunion at Lake Tahoe this year. There were three messages from Kim, two from Marian, five from Hilda, five from Vicki, four from Helen and three from Jackie, all wondering the same thing. How was she getting along with Cade? And there was one urgent message from her editor, asking about the galleys for her next book that were now overdue.

Callie hung up the receiver. She had forgotten all about the galleys. She had intended to bring them with her to the conference so she could finish reading them but, in the rush to get ready, she had left them sitting on her desk. Now they were three days overdue.

Shaking her head, she called Mary Louise and explained, as best she could. As soon as Callie mentioned Cade's name, Mary Louise let out a long "Ahh."

"That explains everything," Mary Louise remarked, "but we need those galleys ASAP."

"I know. Any chance you could overnight them to me here?"

"For you? Yes."

"Thanks, I really appreciate it," Callie said, even though it meant starting over again from page one, something she really didn't look forward to doing, since she had already made changes and corrections to the first four hundred and twenty pages.

"Any chance of getting Cade to New York?"

"No, I'm afraid not."

Mary Louise made a tsking sound. "Too bad. He's perfect for your cover."

"Yes," Callie agreed. "Perfect."

After hanging up the receiver, Callie wandered through the house. At home, when she was too upset to write, she cleaned house and that was what she did now. Kola, obviously missing Jacob, trailed at her heels. She dusted the furniture downstairs, and vacuumed the carpets. She mopped the kitchen and bathroom floors and when she finished doing the downstairs, she went upstairs.

She stood in the hallway a moment and then, unable to resist, she walked down the hallway to Cade's room, opened the door and stepped inside.

It was a large square room. The walls were a pale beige, the spread on the king-size bed was a dark blue-and-beige print, the curtains at the large double window were dark blue without fuss or ruffles.

She wandered through the room, thinking there was little in it that gave any insights into Cade's character. There were no mementos of any kind, no pictures on the walls.

She glanced at the top of the large mahogany dresser. There was a handful of change in an ashtray, a few receipts, a matchbook and a rattle in the shape of a turtle.

She picked it up, wondering if it had some special meaning. Had Jacob made it for Cade?

Kola whined softly from the doorway. Putting the rattle back on the dresser, Callie went downstairs and let the dog out.

She wandered through the house for another twenty minutes and then, unable to stand being away from Cade any longer, she grabbed her handbag and her keys, locked up the house and drove to the hospital.

She found Cade in Jacob's room, asleep in a chair.

Jacob smiled at her when she entered the room.

Callie smiled back. "Some people will do anything to get a little attention," she teased, kissing him on the cheek. "How are you feeling?"

"Like a foolish old man."

Callie pulled a chair up to the side of the bed and took his hand in hers. "You look much better than the last time I saw you."

Jacob grunted.

"How much longer will you have to stay here?"

"The doctor said I can go home tomorrow afternoon."

"That's great." She glanced over at Cade again, noting the dark shadows under his eyes.

Jacob followed her gaze. "He needs you."

Callie looked up, startled. "What?"

"He needs you. He is probably too stubborn to admit it. Perhaps he does not yet even realize it, but it is true. And I think you need him."

"Maybe, but I think we're too different to ever be happy together." It hurt to say the words out loud. And even as she said them, she knew it was true. She wanted marriage and children and happy-ever-after and Cade didn't. He liked being on the go. He didn't want any ties other than the ranch, didn't want to settle down and raise a family. He had told her as much when they first met and he had never said or done anything to make her think he had changed his mind.

He stirred then and she watched him stretch out his long

legs, stretch the kinks from his broad shoulders and back and then bolt upright, his gaze darting toward the bed.

"You're awake," Cade said. He stood, grimacing as he arched his back. "How do you feel?"

"Better than you, I think," Jacob replied.

"Yeah, well, that chair's harder than your head." Cade glanced at Callie. "How long have you been here?"

"Just a few minutes."

"Everything all right at the ranch?"

She nodded. "The animals are all fed."

They stared at each other over Jacob's bed, electricity arcing between them like heat lightning in a storm.

Jacob looked up at them, his gaze moving from one to the other, and then grinned. "Why don't you two go on home, get something to eat."

"I don't want to leave you," Cade said. He spoke to Jacob but he was still watching Callie.

"I'll be fine," Jacob said, making a shooing motion with one hand. "Go home and take a shower, get some rest. I'll see you later."

Callie bent down and kissed the old man on the forehead. "Can I bring you anything?"

"Can you bake cookies?"

"Sure. What kind do you like?"

"Surprise me."

"All right. I'll see you later."

Cade gave his great-grandfather's shoulder a squeeze. "Call me if you need me."

"I will."

Cade followed Callie into the hallway. "No sense both of us driving back to the ranch," he said. "Do you want to take my truck or your car?"

She shrugged. "Doesn't matter to me."

"Let's take your car, then," he said, taking the keys from her hand. "I love driving that T-Bird."

"I wish you loved me." She clapped her hand over her mouth, unable to believe she'd said the words aloud. Eyes wide, she stared at him, wishing the ground would swallow her whole, wishing she was anywhere but here.

"Callie…"

"Don't say anything. Forget what I said." She held out her hand, palm up. "Give me the keys."

"Wait a minute, Red…"

She shook her head, mortified at what she'd said, hurt beyond measure by his reaction to her heartfelt declaration. "Just give me my keys. I'm going home."

"I don't want you to go."

A little spark of hope peeked through her despair. "What *do* you want?"

"I want you to stay here. Why don't you…" He took a deep breath. "Why don't you get rid of your place and move in with me?"

She stared at him, unable to believe they were having this conversation in a hospital parking lot, of all places. "Move in with you?"

"Why not? This isn't the Fifties, you know. Lots of couples live together and no one says anything about it."

"Well, my parents would have plenty to say about it."

"Come on, Red, you're a big girl now. I want you. You want me." He ran his knuckles down her cheek. "Change your mind."

"No."

"Why not? Give me one good reason."

"Because it goes against everything I believe in. I don't want to be a live-in girlfriend. I want a man who wants me forever, a man who isn't afraid of commitment." She lifted her chin and squared her shoulders. "I want a man who isn't afraid to tell the world he loves me, someone who'll ride up and…and carry me off on his horse." She knew she was being ridiculous. This was the twenty-first century, not the 1800s, but she was wound up now, and she couldn't stop. "I want a hero, not some…some hunk who's too stubborn to buy the cow!"

And so saying, she snatched the keys from his hand, turned and ran toward her car. She'd have to remember this, she thought, fighting back her tears. It would make a great scene in a book someday.

Unlocking the door, she slid behind the wheel, slammed down the lock on the door and thrust the key into the ignition.

Cade pounded on the window. "Dammit, Red, wait a minute!"

She didn't say anything, just put the car in gear and jammed her foot down on the gas. Maybe she had been a fool to expect him to say that he loved her, too, but she certainly hadn't expected him to suggest they live together.

She shook her head, slowed the car as she pulled out of the parking lot onto the road. Maybe she had overreacted. Maybe she should have waited to see what else he had to say. Maybe living with him wouldn't have been so bad. Lots of people did it these days and no one gave it any thought. Marian had been living with her boyfriend for three years and they seemed to get along fine. Of course, Callie wondered why they didn't get married, since they were so happy together, but that was none of her business.

Callie eased up on the gas. Maybe she shouldn't have said no. With a shake of her head, she thrust the thought away. Whenever she started thinking like that, her grandmother's adage about men and cows always jumped to the forefront of her mind. It might be old-fashioned advice, but it was still true. She hit her fist on the steering wheel as she recalled Cade's remark that he wasn't going hungry. She should have known right then that they had no future together.

Aside from her own feelings on the subject, how would she explain it to her parents and her grandmother if she moved in with Cade? Her parents would never approve. But, more than that, she couldn't face the disappointment in her grand-mother's eyes. And what if, after a few months, Cade decided he didn't want her to live with him anymore? She couldn't face the humiliation. And she wouldn't be able to face Jacob, either. Even though she had known the old man only a short time, she was fond of him, liked him enough to want his respect.

She parked the car in front of the house and hurried inside, anxious to be packed and gone before Cade got home.

She should have known he wouldn't make things easy on her.

She had barely made it into the house before she heard the sound of a car pull into the yard. With nowhere to run and nowhere to hide, she stood in the middle of the living room and waited.

Chapter Seventeen

Callie's heart skipped a beat as she heard the front door open. She opened her mouth to tell Cade that she was leaving, only it wasn't Cade who stepped into the room. She knew immediately that the couple standing inside the doorway had to be Cade's parents.

The man was a taller, older version of Cade—the same black hair, the same deep brown eyes, the same smooth, copper-hued skin.

· The woman had brown hair so dark it was almost black, brown eyes, clear olive skin and a surprised look on her face. She was the first to speak. "Who are you?"

"Callie Walker. I'm a friend of…of Jacob's."

"Indeed?" The woman's narrowed gaze swept the room. "And where is Jacob?"

"You don't know?" Callie asked.

The woman looked up at her husband. "I told you so. What's wrong?" she asked, looking at Callie again. "What's happened?"

"Jacob had a heart attack. He's in the hospital. Didn't Cade get in touch with you yesterday?"

The man dropped the two bags he was carrying. "My wife had a feeling something was wrong at home. We left a day early. How is Jacob?"

"They said he's going to be all right."

"What are you doing here?" the woman asked suspiciously.

"I've been staying with Cade and Jacob for a few days. I was just about to leave when you arrived."

"I think you'd better go to the hospital with us," the man said.

Callie shook her head. "I was just leaving."

"Not until I find out who you are and what you were doing here."

"I just told you," Callie said indignantly.

"I don't mean to offend you, miss," he said, his body blocking the door, "but you can hardly blame me for being suspicious of finding a strange woman in my grandfather's house."

The woman moved farther into the room and dropped the small carry-on bag she was carrying on the sofa. "We'd better go, Zach. Cade can clear this up."

Callie felt a surge of panic. "I really don't want to see Cade again, if you don't mind. My name is Callie Walker and I'm a romance writer. I've been spending a few days with Cade and Jacob. My clothes are upstairs…" She felt her cheeks grow hot. "In the guest room. You'll find a book I autographed for Jacob on the table beside his bed."

Cade's mother left the room. She returned moments later, Callie's book in her hand.

"I guess she's telling the truth." She opened the book to the last page and showed her husband Callie's photo.

"Sorry to have doubted you," he said. "I'm Cade's father, Zachary, and this is my wife, Luisa."

Callie smiled tentatively. "I'm pleased to meet you."

"We'd better go, Zach."

"Yes. Is there anything you'd like us to tell Cade, Miss Walker?"

"No." She and Cade had said everything there was to say.

Zachary smiled at her. "I'm sorry for thinking you were, well, you know."

Callie nodded. "Can't say as I blame you. I'd be suspicious too if I came home and found a stranger in my house. I hope Jacob will be all right. He's a wonderful man. Please tell him goodbye for me, and thank him for his hospitality."

"I'll do that. Come on, Luisa, we'd better go."

Callie watched them leave, then went upstairs to pack, eager to be gone before Cade returned.

Cade looked up at the sound of footsteps, his first thought that Callie had returned.

"Dad. Mom. How'd you get here so fast?"

"We left yesterday morning," his father said quietly. "Your mother had one of her feelings."

"And I was right. Again." She moved toward the bed where Jacob lay sleeping. "Is he going to be all right?"

"Yeah. The doctors said he can go home tomorrow afternoon."

"How serious was it?" his father asked.

Luisa frowned at her husband. "Any time you wind up in the hospital it's serious." She sat down in the chair beside the bed. "There was a woman at the house."

Cade felt a sharp stab of hope. So, she hadn't left after all. "Callie," he said. "She's been staying with us, looking after Jacob."

"Looking after him? Was he sick before this happened?"

"He had a cold. I suspect he was faking the illness to keep Callie at the ranch."

His parents exchanged glances.

"Why would he want to do that?" his father asked.

"He took to her right away," Cade said evasively. "I think he liked having a woman around the house."

"What about you?" This from his mother.

"She's a redhead and a romance writer," Cade replied, as if that explained everything.

"I think I've read a couple of her books," Luisa remarked.

"So," Cade said, his voice as nonchalant as he could manage, "she's still at the ranch."

"She was leaving when we got there," Zach said, taking the chair on the other side of the bed. "I reckon she's gone by now."

"Oh." Cade swore under his breath. Dammit, he should never have let her go.

"So," his mother said, leaning forward in her chair, "where did you meet her?"

"It's a long story."

"We have plenty of time."

Knowing he'd have to tell them sooner or later, Cade quickly explained how he had found Callie on the side of the road and how Jacob had conned him into taking her to Jackson Hole, then picked up her car, ensuring that she would return to the ranch.

"Sounds like he was doing a little matchmaking," Luisa mused after hearing Cade's story.

"She actually wanted you to pose for one of her covers?" This from his father, who was, by the looks of him, doing all he could not to laugh.

"I think you should have done it," Luisa said.

Cade and his father both stared at her. "Are you out of your mind?" Cade exclaimed. "I'd be the laughingstock of the whole town."

Luisa shrugged. "Maybe, but I'll bet there's not a man in town who wouldn't jump at the chance."

Zachary shook his head. "You made the right decision, son."

"He made the wrong decision."

Three pairs of eyes swung in Jacob's direction.

"How do you figure, *Tunkashila?*" Cade asked.

"It would have given you more time with Callie, for one thing." He pinned Cade with a stern look. "Now you have lost her."

"She didn't want *me,*" he muttered. "She wanted a cover model."

Jacob snorted derisively. "Where is the young man I taught to see the world? The one who could track a deer and follow a fox back to its den? Have you gone suddenly blind? I am an old man, but I saw the way *she* looked at you." Jacob paused and took a breath. "I saw the way *you* looked at her."

Cade shook his head. "Grandfather…"

Jacob glanced past Cade. "Zachary," he said frowning. "What are you doing here?"

"You know Luisa. She had a feeling something was wrong and insisted we come home early."

"Ah, the witch at work." A smile took the sting from Jacob's words.

Rising, Luisa took his hand in hers. "Say what you want, old man," she said, her eyes bright. "But I was right again, wasn't I?"

Giving her hand a squeeze, Jacob nodded. "I'm glad you're here. Maybe you can talk some sense into your son."

"I wish I could," Luisa said, throwing a glance at Cade. "I'm beginning to think it's a lost cause. I was hoping for grandchildren while I'm still young enough to hold them."

"Come on, Mom," Cade said, "Gail's given you four in the last five years."

Luisa nodded. "But she can't have any more."

"Four's plenty."

"Stop worrying, Luisa," Jacob said, smiling faintly. "I saw Callie in a vision the night before she came to the ranch. The boy can fight it all he wants, but she is meant to be his."

Cade glared at his great-grandfather. "Is that so?"

"You know it's true," Jacob said, tapping his heart, "in here."

There was no arguing with that. As much as he wanted to, Cade knew, in his heart and soul, that Callie was the only woman for him. He loved her spunk, her willingness to trust him. He loved the way she made him feel like smiling, the way her curvy little figure molded so perfectly to his own. Jacob was right. She was the only woman for him. He just hoped he hadn't realized it too late.

Rising, he dropped a quick kiss on his mother's cheek, shook his dad's hand, squeezed Jacob's shoulder. Maybe, if he hurried, he could catch her before it was too late.

Chapter Eighteen

She told herself she wouldn't cry. She. Would. Not. He wasn't worth a single one of her tears, let alone the torrent that was making it almost impossible to see the road ahead. And yet, she couldn't stop crying.

How could she have been such a fool? It had been Jacob who suggested Cade take her to Jackson Hole, Jacob who had brought her car back to the ranch in hopes of keeping them together a little longer. Jacob who had wanted the two of them to be together. Given his druthers, Cade would have sent her on her way the day after they met.

Ah, well, wasn't that why she wrote fiction? At least when she wrote a book, she was assured of a happy ending. But there was no happy ending for her, not this time. At least the trip hadn't been a total waste of time. She had won a coveted award, she'd been able to spend time on a real ranch, she had met Jacob Red Crow…she sniffed back her tears. He would make a great character in a book some day. She would have to remember to send him a copy when it was published.

She drove until dark, then pulled into the first motel she saw. There was a small restaurant nearby and though she wasn't really hungry, she didn't feel like sitting alone in a strange room.

She ordered an egg salad sandwich and a chocolate shake and, after taking a few bites, found she was hungry after all.

"Must not be true love," she muttered, licking a bit of egg from her lower lip. "Brokenhearted heroines never have an appetite."

Back in her motel room, she took a quick shower, slipped into her nightgown, then worked on her current work in progress for an hour before shutting down her laptop and slipping under the covers.

Cade's image immediately rose in her mind. Drat the man! He was harder to shake than the twenty-four-hour flu.

Flopping over on her stomach, she banished him from her mind, but to no avail. He rode into her dreams astride a huge white horse that was the perfect complement to his dark skin and long black hair. He rode majestically, his carriage as proud as that of the stallion he rode. She stood in the middle of a clearing clad in a long green dress and a pair of half-boots, her hair blown by a hot summer breeze, her heart pounding with trepidation as the horse pranced toward her.

Filled with a sudden nameless fear, she glanced around, startled to find Vicki and Helen, Kim and Jackie, Marian and Hilda, all standing in a circle around her, all dressed in doe-skin tunics and moccasins. Jacob was there, too, clad in buckskins and a warbonnet whose feathers dragged on the ground. And, oddly, off in the distance, she saw her editor.

Callie started to run toward Vicki for help but suddenly Cade was there, between them. He leaned toward her, one bronzed, well-muscled arm closing around her waist. He lifted her easily and set her on the horse in front of him and then, with a shrill, ululating cry, he carried her into the trees beyond the clearing.

Reining the horse to a halt, he spoke to her in a language she couldn't understand but knew was Lakota. Dismounting, he lifted her from the back of the stallion, let her body slide intimately against his own as he set her on her feet.

She looked up at him, her heart pounding, waiting, waiting, for him to say the words she longed to hear.

His dark eyes gazed deeply into hers. He stroked her cheek with his knuckles in a gesture that was so tender, so endearing, she felt tears sting her eyes.

"Cade."

He spoke to her then. She leaned forward, unable to hear what he was saying as a car raced by, its horn blaring.

She woke with a start, Cade's name on her lips, disappointment settling like a rock in her heart when she realized it had all been a dream.

An hour later, after a quick breakfast in the restaurant, she was on the road again.

Her condo looked smaller than she remembered it. A fine layer of dust covered everything. There were nine new messages on her answering machine.

Feeling less than happy to be there, she carried her luggage into the bedroom. Lacking the energy or the desire to unpack, she dropped everything but her laptop on the floor.

Her refrigerator was empty, which meant she was going to have to go to the store.

She needed to go to the post office and pick up her mail.

She had to finish her galleys.

She needed to do her laundry and dust the furniture.

It could all wait while she read her e-mail.

Booting up her computer, she went through her e-mail, deleting what seemed like a ton of spam, and then she opened one from Vicki. It was a photo of Callie and Cade. Underneath the picture, Vicki had written "The future Mr. and Mrs. Kills Thunder" with about a dozen question marks after it.

"Very funny," she muttered, but she didn't delete the photo.

She read the rest of her e-mail, answered her fan letters, sent a note to her editor and her agent, telling them that she had made it safely home.

She hadn't given Cade her e-mail address. Had he noticed it was in the back of her book? She hadn't thought to give him her phone number or home address, either, nor had she written his down. Perhaps it was just as well. If she had his phone number, she might be tempted to call, just to see how Jacob was, of course.

Muttering "Stop it!" under her breath, she grabbed her car keys and headed for the store. Not only was she out of bread and milk, she was out of chocolate! And if she'd ever needed her favorite comfort food, it was now.

Cade leaned against the bar, one boot heel hooked over the rail, a glass of whiskey, untouched, in his hand, as he watched Housley and Norton try to pick up a couple of women at the other end of the bar. He had bet each man five dollars that they couldn't score.

"Hey, Thunder, long time no see."

He turned his head to find Molly What's-her-name standing at his elbow. "How you doing, Moll?" Clad in a slinky black top that looked two sizes too small, skintight black jeans and a pair of high-heeled boots, she was dressed to draw the attention of every man in the place

"Fine, as always. I haven't seen you over at the Spur lately," she said, faking a pout.

"I've been busy out at the ranch." He grinned inwardly as Housley and Norton both struck out.

She ran one bloodred fingernail down his cheek as she purred, "Well, cowboy, you don't look very busy tonight." She leaned toward him, giving him a clear view of her ample cleavage.

Cade drew his attention from his two buddies and focused on Molly. Hard to believe he had once thought her pretty, or considered taking her out. Looking at her now, he wondered what he had ever seen in her. Her straw-blond hair was black at the roots, her lipstick was a too-bright orange, her lashes were caked with mascara.

He swore under his breath. Molly was here and she was more than willing, but he no longer found her even remotely attractive. Unfortunately, try as he might, he couldn't work up one iota of interest in the woman who was standing so close to him it looked as if they were joined at the hip. And even though he had come in here determined to ease his ache in the arms of another woman, it was impossible to banish Callie's image from his heart or his mind. If she had worn makeup, he hadn't been aware of it other than a touch of pink at her lips. Molly looked suddenly cheap and overblown when compared to Callie's wholesome sensuality.

Molly put her hand on his arm and gave it a squeeze. "How about buying a lonely girl a drink?"

"Sure." He signaled for the bartender. There had been a time when he wouldn't have thought twice about taking what Molly was so clearly offering. It would have been wham, bam, thank you, ma'am. But that had been before Red entered his life and made him start thinking about marriage and kids and settling down with one woman, forever.

Looking crestfallen, Housley and Norton sauntered over a few minutes later. Wordlessly, they each slapped a five-dollar bill on the bar.

"You win," Housley muttered.

"Yeah," Norton said glumly.

"I'll bet you couldn't score with either one of them, either," Housley said, a challenge in his voice.

"Yeah." Norton reached into his pocket and slapped another bill on the bar. "Here's five that says you can't do any better than we did."

Housley's expression brightened as he dropped a bill on top of Norton's. "I want a piece of that."

"Forget it, fellas." Cade handed his drink to Housley, then took Molly's hand from his arm and placed it in Norton's. "Have fun, kids. I'm going home."

"Now?" Norton exclaimed. "It's the shank of the evening."

"Why do you want to go home?" Housley asked, staring at him in disbelief. "It's barely nine-thirty."

"Way past my bedtime, fellas. So long, Molly."

And so saying, Cade skirted the smoky dance floor and headed for the door, leaving the three of them staring after him.

He paused at the door, then stepped outside and drew in a long breath of cool Montana air.

Grinning, he closed the door behind him and as he did so, he knew he was closing the door on that part of his life for good.

Sliding behind the wheel of his truck, he rolled the window down and drove home.

The following evening, Cade leaned against Clyde's corral, one booted foot on the bottom rail, his arms dangling over the top. Without Red, his life seemed to have lost its meaning. The ranch didn't seem the same either. In the last five days, he had thrown himself into sprucing up the old place. He had painted the barn, repaired the corral gate, fixed the squeaky hinge on the back door. Jacob had asked if they were expecting company. Cade had growled at the old man and then felt guilty as hell. His great-grandfather had only been home from the hospital for a few days and though Jacob insisted he felt fine, Cade thought a good wind would blow the old man away. He had turned down three jobs since Jacob came home from the hospital, afraid to leave the old man alone. Jacob had reminded him that Zach and Luisa were only a phone call away, but as far as Cade was concerned, it was too far.

If he'd been honest with himself, Cade would have admitted Jacob wasn't the only reason he didn't want to be away from the ranch right now. Every time the phone rang, he felt a quick rush of adrenaline, one instant of hope that it might be Red calling, if not to talk to him, then at least to ask how Jacob was. But she never called, not once. Late one night, he had given in to the temptation and called information, only to discover that her phone number was unlisted.

Filled with resentment, he had gone online and looked up her Web page, felt his heart speed up when her site loaded and he saw her photo smiling at him. And her e-mail address was there at the bottom of the page.

He had written her a short note, debated how to sign it and then deleted it. If she had wanted to hear from him, she would have given him her phone number.

He slammed his fist on the edge of the rail. His name was in the phone book. If she wanted to hear from him, she could just call him up.

It didn't help that, every time his parents came over, his mother asked if he had heard from Callie.

"You could always write her a fan letter, you know," Luisa had suggested just the day before.

Cade had glared at his mother.

"I think that's a fine idea," Jacob said. "I read her latest book. It was the best one yet."

"Then *you* write to her," Cade had said, and stomped out of the house.

Later that night, after his parents had gone home and Jacob was asleep, Cade had been unable to resist going online again. Feeling like some fool schoolboy or some romance groupie, he had sat there for almost an hour, staring at her photo and wondering how it had all gone so wrong so fast.

The next day, he went online and found Vicki Brown's e-mail address.

The day after that, he picked up a one-way run to Los Angeles.

Chapter Nineteen

"Vicki, would you just listen to me for a minute..."

Callie drummed her fingers on the desktop, wishing Vicki would take no for an answer, but every time Callie said no, Vicki came up with another reason why they should meet at the park the following afternoon.

"All right, all right," she said in exasperation. "I'll go."

"You won't be sorry," Vicki said. "Should I pick you up?"

"What's the matter? Don't you trust me?"

"I'd tell you, but you wouldn't like my answer. Honestly, Callie, you've got to happy up."

"I'm happy."

"Uh-huh."

"I know what you're thinking. You're thinking I should call him. Well..."

"No, no," Vicki said quickly, "I think that would be a terrible idea."

"You do?" Callie asked, unable to keep the surprise out of her voice. "Why?"

"Because...I...you said...well, I just do. Who needs a cowboy truck driver, even if he is gorgeous."

I do, Callie thought.

"Well, I've got to go," Vicki said. "This darn book won't write itself. Sometimes I think I should have gone into another line of work."

Callie laughed. "I know what you mean. I'm bogged down in the middle of my latest. At least I finally got through the galleys for my next one." She blew out a sigh. "I've read that thing so darn many times, I don't know if it's any good or not."

"You always say that," Vicki said, laughing. "I'm sure it's great, like always."

"I hope so." As always, thinking of her next book brought Cade to mind. But then, it seemed everything she did or thought about brought Cade to mind.

"See you tomorrow," Vicki said. "Oh, I'm dressing up."

"Dressing up? To go to the park?"

"Well, I thought we'd go to lunch afterwards. I told Jackie and the others that we'd be in town and we thought it might be fun to get together. After all, we haven't seen each other since the conference."

"All right. See you tomorrow. Bye."

"Bye."

Callie hung up the receiver. It would be good to see Vicki and the others. They tried to get together at least once a month for lunch or dinner. It was a great opportunity to brag or complain about rewrites, covers both good and bad, galleys, contracts, editors, agents, convict mail, bad reviews and any and all of the other ups and downs inherent in the wonderful world of publishing.

For the first time in days, she found herself looking forward to getting out of the house.

Dearmond Park was located on a quiet side street in an older part of the city. There was a large stable across the street where horses could be boarded or rented. Callie watched a young girl wearing a helmet ride by on a pretty little gray pony. Maybe one of these days she would come down here and rent a horse, Callie thought, remembering how much she had enjoyed riding with Cade. Of course, it wouldn't be as much fun if he weren't with her.

She glanced at her watch, wondering what was keeping Vicki. It was unusual for her friend to be late; she was usually the first to arrive whenever they planned to get together.

With a sigh, she turned her attention back to the arena, visible beyond a chain-link fence. A man was riding inside, putting a big bald-faced black horse through its paces. The man was a good rider, she thought, but nowhere near the horseman that Cade was.

Cade. There he was, in her thoughts again. Was she doomed to spend the rest of her life thinking of him at every turn? She had almost called him last night on the pretense of asking after Jacob. It would have been the perfect excuse for making the call. She had even gone so far as to dial his number and then had hung up on the first ring, afraid that if she heard his voice, she might have been tempted beyond endurance to forget her upbringing and her grandmother's oft repeated words and tell Cade Kills Thunder that she had changed her mind, that she would move in with him or do anything else he wanted because she missed him so darn much!

Of course, she was glad now that she hadn't let the call go through. Wasn't she?

Callie glanced at her watch again. Vicki was almost fifteen minutes late, which was highly unusual. Perhaps something had detained her and she couldn't make it, but if that was the case, surely she would have called. With a sigh, Callie decided to give Vicki five more minutes. If she didn't show up by then, Callie would just go home. She hadn't wanted to come here anyway.

She was watching the man in the arena when she felt a sudden shiver down her spine. Frowning, she glanced right and left and then, hearing the sound of hoofbeats behind her, she turned around.

And almost fainted at the sight that met her eyes.

A tall, dark-skinned man was riding toward her on a big white horse, a horse that pranced and tossed its head as if it was aware that she was watching. The man was clad in a breechclout, fringed leggings and moccasins. He wore an eagle feather in his long black hair and carried a feathered lance in his right hand. There was a slash of black paint across one cheek, another zigzagged down his broad chest.

Callie stared at him. Blinked, and blinked again. It couldn't be. Impossible as it seemed, she was looking at the cover of her next book come to life.

Even more unbelievable was the fact that the rider was Cade.

He drew back on the reins and the big horse reared, forelegs pawing the air, before dropping back on the ground.

Cade sat there a moment, looking as proud and untamed as the stallion. Then he swung agilely to the ground and walked toward her, his long legs eating up the distance between them. The horse trailed behind him.

"What are you doing here?" she asked breathlessly. "How did you find me? Whose horse is that?"

"You ask too many questions," he said, his voice as arrogant as his stance.

When she started to object, he dropped the reins and swept her into his arms, his mouth covering hers. At the touch of his lips, all thought of protesting melted away like morning dew.

He was here. What else mattered?

Her arms went around his waist, her fingertips encountering sun-warmed skin. She ran her hands up and down his back, loving the feel of his heated skin beneath her palms, loving the hard length of his body pressed ever so intimately against her own.

She moaned softly as he deepened the kiss. His tongue dueled with hers, sending frissons of desire running down her spine to pool in the core of her being. When she came up for a breath, she didn't even care that a crowd had gathered around them. She had waited too long for this moment, this man. It never occurred to her to object when he kissed her again, and then again.

Her legs felt a little shaky when he finally released her. Not certain they would support her, she kept one arm around his waist.

"Cade, what are you doing here?" she asked again.

A slow smile spread over his lips. "What do you think?"

"If I knew, I wouldn't have asked."

"I missed you. I missed you so much I even read that book you signed for Jacob. When I got to the end and I saw your picture…" He lifted one shoulder and let it fall. "I knew my life wouldn't amount to a hill of beans unless I had a pretty little redheaded woman to share it with me."

She stared up at him, every nerve and cell in her body waiting for the words she longed to hear.

"I came to tell you I'd pose for the cover of your book if that's what you want…"

"You will? Really?"

"Really." He jerked a thumb over his shoulder. "Ask your editor."

"She's here?" Callie peered around Cade, unable to believe her eyes when she saw Mary Louise standing a few feet away, a photographer at her elbow.

"I don't believe it."

He placed a finger over her lips. "I'm not through. I asked you before, now I'm asking you again. Will you come and live with me…" His words trailed off and he took a deep breath.

Disappointment cooled her excitement, smothered her foolish hopes. Silly romantic that she was, she had been ex-

pecting a proposal, not a proposition. She bit down on her
lower lip, wondering if she was strong enough to refuse him
a second time. How could she ever let him go again?

"...as my wife."

She stared up at him, speechless. Had she heard him right?
Afraid she might have imagined those three words, she stood
there, mute.

"Hey, Red? Is that a yes?"

She nodded. "Yes! Oh, yes! Oh, Cade!"

Laughing and crying, she threw her arms around his neck.
If this was a dream, she never, ever wanted to wake up.

And then Vicki was there, along with Jackie, Helen, Marian, Kim and Hilda, all of them hugging her and congratulat-
ing her at the same time.

When the first wave of excitement died down, Mary Louise informed Callie that they were going to shoot the cover
for her next book there, in the park, right then, and that they
wanted her to be the female model.

"Me?" Callie exclaimed. "But I'm too short. My hair's the
wrong color and..."

Mary Louise waved aside her protests. "Vito's the best
cover artist in the business, honey. He can make you taller, en-
hance your cleavage, change the color of your hair and
eyes..."

"Callie, you've got to do this!" Vicki insisted. "You'll hate
yourself if you don't, you know you will."

"Absolutely," Jackie said. "You'll be great!"

But it was Cade who convinced her. "I won't do it with
anyone but you." His dark eyes moved over her, bringing a
flush to her cheeks. "What do you say, Red?"

What else could she say, but, "Let's do it."

Callie had seen them do cover shoots before but she had
never, in her wildest fantasies, imagined that she would actually *be* on a cover, let alone on a cover for one of her own
books. Mary Louise had brought an old-fashioned dress for

Callie to wear and as she posed with Cade, she realized it was her dream come true—a wild Indian on a white horse, herself in a long green calico dress, her friends surrounding her.

She couldn't remember when she'd ever had quite so much fun. Following the photographer's directions, she stood facing Cade, her head tilted back a little so she could look up into his face. They posed on the horse, with Cade sitting behind her, one arm around her waist. They posed lying on the grass in each other's arms. They posed with Cade standing behind her, one hand resting possessively on her shoulder. They posed with Callie looking away, a wistful expression on her face, while Cade gazed down at her. Later, they took several photographs of Cade standing and then sitting on the horse, alone. Callie took the photographer aside and asked him to send her copies of the pictures, especially the ones of Cade on the horse.

When they were through with the shoot, there was a round of applause from the onlookers; then, after Cade and Callie changed clothes in the photographer's rented motor home, Mary Louise took them all out to dinner.

It was after ten when Cade and Callie finally found themselves alone in her condo.

Cade glanced around, curious to see where she lived. The rooms were large, the walls painted a soft robin's-egg blue. The carpets were off-white, the furniture a mixture of antique oak and wicker. There were posters of some of her book covers on the walls in the hallway. A bookshelf in the den held copies of all her books, some in foreign languages, as well as the awards she had won. There were plants everywhere.

Callie followed him from room to room, saying little.

Returning to the living room, Cade drew her into his arms. "Tell me," he said. "Tell me you missed me as much as I missed you."

"I missed you dreadfully." She brushed a lock of hair from his brow. "I can't believe you came after me." She grinned up at him, remembering how surprised she had been to see him. "And on a white horse yet. My hero."

He grunted softly. "I wouldn't have done a stunt like that for anyone but you, and you know it. I'll probably have to leave home when that book comes out. I know I'll never live it down." He shook his head ruefully. "The other truckers are never gonna let me forget it. And I don't even want to think about what Housley and Dockstader and Norton are gonna say. Especially Norton."

She smiled up at him, her eyes filled with love. "I'll call Mary Louise tomorrow," she said. "I'll tell her you've changed your mind and to schedule a new shoot, or to recycle an old cover. But, one way or another, I'm going to have copies of those pictures, even if no one ever sees them but me."

Cade looked down at her. She never failed to surprise him, he thought. She had done everything but get down on her knees and beg him to pose for her cover, and now that he'd done it, she was letting him off the hook, no muss, no fuss.

"No way, Red. This may be my one claim to fame." Reaching into his pants' pocket, he withdrew a small gray velvet box and handed it to her.

Heart pounding, Callie lifted the lid. Inside lay the most beautiful diamond ring she had ever seen.

"I'll try to make you happy, Red."

"You already make me happy."

Cade placed his finger beneath her chin and lifted her head, his dark eyes burning into hers. "I love you."

Tears of happiness welled in her eyes. "I love you more."

"Name the day and the place, darlin'," Cade said, taking the ring from the box and placing the ring on her finger, "and I'll be there, in a tux or a breechclout…" He grinned down at her. "Or nothing at all."

Chapter Twenty

Because she had met Cade in Montana, Callie decided that was where she wanted to be married, the sooner the better. She put her condo up for sale, pleased when it sold in the first week. She asked Vicki to be her maid of honor, and Hilda, Marian, Kim, Helen and Jackie to be her bridesmaids. They spent one whole Saturday shopping for a wedding dress and the next weekend looking for dresses for Vicki and the others, finally deciding on a pale blue silk for Vicki and a darker blue for the bridesmaids.

The girls gave her a surprise shower the week after Cade went back to Montana. She had hated to see him go, but she knew he was needed at home to look after Jacob and the ranch. And, of course, he had to rent a tux and round up a best man and a few groomsmen.

Callie wasn't the least bit surprised when most of the presents she received from her closest friends turned out to be see-through nightgowns and edible underwear. Of course, she received candy dishes, pots and pans, and linens, as well.

She took the girls to lunch the following week and then, all too soon, it was time for her to leave. The girls helped her pack, all lamenting the fact that she would be moving so far away.

"Promise you'll keep in touch," Vicki said.

"You know I will. And there's always e-mail," Callie reminded them. "And conferences practically every month of the year where we can get together."

"Maybe we should all move to Montana," Marian suggested. "Maybe that's where all the good-looking hunks are hiding out."

"Sounds like a good idea to me," Kim agreed. "Maybe Cade has a cousin or two we don't know about."

"I still can't believe he showed up in the park on a horse," Jackie said. "That was so romantic."

"I can't believe you're flying to Montana," Helen said, folding one of Callie's sweaters. "It must be love."

It was difficult for Callie to tell them all goodbye when the time came. Cade had taken her car to Montana, so the girls drove her to the airport, assuring her there was nothing to worry about, but it had been Callie's eagerness to be with Cade as soon as possible that had convinced her to take a plane, "just this once."

He was waiting for her at the depot when she arrived. She spotted him immediately. He stood head and shoulders above everyone else and she felt a surge of pleasure at knowing he was hers, only hers, and that she would soon be his wife.

She ran toward him and he scooped her up into his arms. "Hey, Red."

She smiled up at him, her eyes closing as he lowered his head to kiss her. Pleasure moved through her, hot and slow, like honey on a warm summer day.

She nibbled his lower lip. "I missed you."

"I missed you, too. Come on, let's get your luggage and get out of here."

She couldn't seem to keep her hands off him as they drove to the ranch. She ran her knuckles over his cheek, brushed a lock of hair from his brow, rested her hand on his thigh, her fingertips lightly kneading the muscle there.

"You'd better stop that," he warned in a low growl, "or we're gonna wind up in another ditch."

When they drove up the road to the ranch, it was like coming home. "How's Jacob?"

"Much better. And eager to see you."

"I missed him, too. He's such a dear old man."

"And a hell of a matchmaker."

"That, too," she agreed with a grin.

Cade's parents were there to greet her. Zach and Luisa welcomed her with open arms and insisted that she and Cade hold the reception at their ranch. Callie wished her own parents had been as accepting of Cade as his parents were of her. She had called her mom and dad the day after Cade proposed. Her father had thought it was wonderful that she'd finally decided to settle down, though he remarked that he'd always hoped she would marry a lawyer or a doctor. Her mother had seemed a little apprehensive to learn her future son-in-law was not only an Indian and a truck driver, but that he had recently embarked on a new career as a cover model.

Callie's heart swelled with affection as she hugged Jacob. She was glad to see that he looked marvelously fit in spite of his recent illness.

Holding her at arm's length, he gave her a knowing smile. "I told Cade you were the one," he said. "Even before I saw you, I knew you were the one."

"How did you know?"

"The night before Cade brought you home, I saw you in a dream."

The next few weeks passed in a blur. They found a lovely old church for the wedding. It was set among towering pines and lovely ferns, with a large stained glass window behind the altar.

Her parents arrived a few days before the wedding and, thankfully, all the parents managed to get along.

Vicki and the rest of the girls arrived the day after Callie's parents and the next two days passed amid a flurry of wedding rehearsals and dinners. Cade's best man gave him a bachelor party and Luisa gave a shower for Callie, which gave her a chance to meet the other members of Cade's family, including his sister and her family, as well as a large number of aunts, uncles and cousins. They were a friendly, generous bunch and she loved them all immediately, though she wasn't sure she would ever learn all their names or remember who was married to whom, and which kids belonged where.

And suddenly, amidst all the planning and the shopping, the big day was upon them.

Callie woke late after a restless night. How could she be expected to sleep when she was getting married the next day?

Upon waking, her first thought was that it was her wedding day. And what a beautiful day it was. The sky was a clear bright blue; the weather promised to be warm.

A glance at the clock showed she had less than an hour and a half to eat, shower, and dress.

She had no sooner gotten out of bed than there was a knock on her door.

"Callie, are you up?"

It was her mother.

"Yes," she called. "Come in."

Kaye Walker smiled as she entered the room, a cup of coffee in one hand. "Today's the day," she remarked, handing the cup to her daughter.

Callie nodded, surprised to find there were butterflies in her stomach. But she supposed that was to be expected. Weren't brides supposed to be nervous?

"Cade's downstairs having breakfast. I wasn't sure if you wanted to eat downstairs or not."

Callie shook her head. "It's bad luck for the groom to see the bride before the wedding."

With a grin, Kaye checked her hair in the mirror. "I wasn't sure if girls nowadays still believed that."

"Well, this one does. Does he seem nervous?"

"No more than you. Why don't you take a shower and I'll go down and fix you something to eat."

"Thanks, Mom."

Kaye gave her a hug, tears shimmering in her eyes, then left the room.

Callie took a quick shower and when she returned to her room, her mother was there.

"I made your favorite," Kaye said. "French toast."

"Thanks, Mom, but I don't think I'm very hungry."

"You'd better eat something. I remember my wedding day. I didn't eat, either, and you could hear my stomach growling all through the ceremony."

"You're making that up!"

"It's the truth. Ask your father."

With a chuckle, Callie decided she'd better eat.

She thought about Cade as she dressed, wondering what he would think of the lacy white underwear she had bought with him in mind. It was little more than a whisper of sheer white silk.

Her dress was long, with a flared skirt, a round neck, fitted sleeves, and a short train. Tiny seed pearls and brilliants made the gown shimmer when she moved. She stepped into a pair of white heels; her mother placed a shoulder-length veil on her head, and they were ready to go.

Callie took a last glance at herself in the mirror. Her eyes were sparkling, her cheeks were rosy. She thought of Cade again and felt beautiful.

Her father was waiting for her at the foot of the stairs. "You look wonderful, princess," he said, kissing her cheek. "Cade's a lucky man."

"Thank you, Daddy. You're looking mighty fine yourself."

"Are you ready?"

She nodded.

Moments later, they were at the church. There was a flurry of excitement as she entered the bride's room, tons of hugs and good wishes from Jackie, Vicki, Helen, Kim, Hilda and Marian.

"Wow," Vicki said, "I don't know if it's being in love or that dress, but you look fantastic, girlfriend."

"I'll say," Hilda agreed.

"Brides are always beautiful," Callie said.

Kaye came up behind her to straighten her veil. "Not as beautiful as you are," she said, giving her a squeeze.

"They're ready for us," Jackie said.

"Are you ready?" Hilda asked. "Do you have something old?"

"My watch," Callie said.

"Something new?" This from Helen.

"Everything I'm wearing," Callie replied with a grin.

"Something borrowed?" Kim queried.

"Mom's hanky."

"What about something blue?" Marian asked.

Callie's eyes widened. "I don't have anything blue."

"Here," Vicki said. Plucking a blue rosette from her hair, she lifted Callie's veil and pinned the rosette in her hair where it was barely noticeable.

Kaye kissed her daughter on the cheek, then hurried out of the room. Callie and the others followed a few moments later.

"Are you sure about this?" her father asked as they took their place in the vestibule.

"Very sure."

The music changed and the familiar strains of "Here Comes the Bride" filled the air.

Her father patted her hand. "Here we go."

Callie watched Vicki walk down the aisle, followed by the

others. As she approached the door, she felt her heart skip a beat as she got her first glimpse of Cade. Good Lord, she had thought he was the most gorgeous thing she had ever seen when she saw him in that café dressed in jeans and a cowboy shirt. She had been certain he was the sexiest thing on two legs when she saw him in a breechclout and moccasins astride a white stallion. But in a tux, the man defied description.

As though he knew she was watching him, Cade turned his head ever so slightly. He smiled then, a smile that was meant for her alone. She felt the heat of his gaze burn into her and through her, and then her father was walking her down the aisle. She didn't hear the music, was hardly aware of people rising on both sides as she passed by. All she could see was Cade waiting for her at the altar. Never had the words tall, dark and handsome been more appropriate.

The minister spoke, and her father placed her hand in Cade's. Hers trembled slightly; Cade's fingers were warm and firm as they closed around hers.

He whispered, "Hey, Red," his smile melting her heart as his hand tightened around hers, and then they faced the minister, listening to his counsel and words of advice on marriage, repeating the time-honored vows that joined them together as husband and wife.

"You may kiss your bride."

Slowly, almost reverently, Cade lifted her veil. He gazed down at her for stretched seconds, as though he wanted to imprint this moment forever in his memory, and then he lowered his head and claimed his first kiss as her husband. The warmth of his lips, the rightness of standing in his embrace in the presence of her friends and family, filled her with a sense of peace unlike anything she had ever known. Then there was only the touch of his lips on hers as he deepened the kiss.

She was breathless, her legs a little shaky, when he finally let her go.

"Friends, relatives, honored guests, may I present Mr. and Mrs. Cade Kills Thunder."

Hand in hand, surrounded by smiles and good wishes, a few happy tears and scattered applause, Cade and Callie left the church.

Outside, there were hugs from friends and family and then Cade handed her into the limo for the drive to his parents' ranch.

As soon as the door closed, Cade drew Callie into his arms and kissed her, hard and long. She melted against him, her heart pounding.

"Happy?" he asked between hot, hungry kisses.

"Oh, yes." She held him at arm's length for a moment. "Would you have really worn a breechcloth?" she asked, grinning.

His gaze caressed her. "What do you think?"

"I think every woman in the church would have swooned, and…ohhh, Cade." She moaned softly, leaning into him as his hand cupped and caressed her breast. "That feels so good."

"You feel so good."

She ran her hand along the inside of his thigh, felt his muscles tense.

"Watch out, Red," he warned, his voice husky. "Don't tease the tiger."

She laughed out loud, gasped as he pressed her down on the seat, his upper body covering hers, his tongue tickling her ear.

"Cade…" She pushed her hands against his chest. "You're mussing me."

He looked down at her, one brow arched. "Do you care?"

"Not really, but…" Her protests were smothered in the heat of his kisses.

Caught up in a haze of passion, she didn't realize the limo had come to a halt until someone opened the door. Blinking against the light, she felt her cheeks grow hot when Vicki leaned inside.

"Hey! Are you two ever coming out of there?"

Cade muttered an oath as he sat up, all too aware that what he was feeling for his new bride was blatantly obvious. "You go ahead," he said.

Callie grinned a knowing grin.

A moment later, the driver opened the door on her side and she climbed out, to be quickly surrounded by her girlfriends.

"Geez, Callie, can't you wait until you get to the hotel?" Hilda asked, laughing out loud.

"Or at least until you make it into the house?" Jackie added.

Callie pressed a hand to her burning cheeks. "Oh, hush, you two."

The rest of the day passed in a blur. There was the reception line, followed by a lavish buffet supper, then dancing under the stars and the cutting of the cake. Through it all, she found herself counting the hours until she could be alone with Cade. She touched him at every opportunity, unable to believe he was really hers, that they would be spending the rest of their lives together.

She danced with her father, with Cade's father, with Jacob. And then, one more dance with Cade before they snuck away to change clothes. Cade had offered to take her anywhere she wanted to go for her honeymoon and she had picked Hawaii, but they were spending tonight in the Rose Room at the Bennett House Country Inn.

Callie slipped into a pale blue linen dress and matching heels, aware of Cade's intense gaze as she changed. She could hardly wait until they were alone, until she could hold him and kiss him and explore that hard-muscled body to her heart's content.

As if reading her mind, he grinned at her. "Soon, darlin'," he murmured, dropping butterfly kisses along the length of her neck. "Soon."

They left amid a shower of hugs, kisses and good wishes,

tin cans trailing behind the limo, the words Just Married written in large white letters across the back window.

Callie smiled at Cade, thinking that, at last, the reality of her life was better than the fiction that filled the pages of her books.

Chapter Twenty-One

"Did I tell you how pretty you look?" Cade asked as he carried her across the threshold of the Rose Room.

Callie shook her head, thinking how wonderful it felt to be in his arms. They had checked in to the Bennett House Country Inn just a few moments earlier.

The lady at the desk had beamed at them. "You're newlyweds, aren't you? I can always tell."

Cade gave the door a kick with his boot heel, cocooning them in the shadows of the room. "I don't think I've ever seen anything more beautiful than the way you looked walking down the aisle. All I could think of was that you were mine." He brushed a kiss across her lips. "And that I almost let you go." He kissed her again, longer and deeper this time.

"I love you, Cade."

His gaze moved over her, hot and hungry, filled with love and desire. "How much?"

"More than anything in the world."

"More than chocolate?"

"More than hot fudge."

He grinned at that, and she smiled. "Don't you want to put me down? I must be getting heavy."

"You, heavy?" He laughed softly. "I could hold you like this all night."

"Really?" She batted her eyelashes at him. "Won't it be kind of hard for us to…you know."

"Hard?" he asked, a wicked gleam in his eye. "Do you want me to show you what hard is?"

"Hah! I bet I can guess what it is."

"Can you?"

"I'm a romance writer, you know."

He laughed out loud at that. Lowering her feet to the floor, he held her body pressed close to his, letting her feel the hard heat of his desire.

"Oh, my," she murmured, doing her best Mae West impression, "is that a gun in your pocket, or are you just glad to see me?"

"I intend to see you, all right," he said, his voice a low growl. "All of you."

Reaching around behind her, he began to unzip her dress.

Callie's heart skipped a beat as his fingertips brushed her skin. Faster than she would have thought possible, he had her out of her dress and slip. She couldn't help blushing as his gaze moved over her, lingering on the lacy froth of satin and lace that covered her breasts.

"You really are beautiful, Red," he murmured.

"So are you." Eager to see all of him, she removed his jacket and shirt, unfastened his belt.

He pulled off his boots and socks. She kicked off her shoes. Slowly, so slowly, he peeled off her nylons, his hands sliding slowly, sensuously down her thighs, her calves, her ankles.

Rising, he drew her into his embrace again. She was surprised at the tremor in his arms.

"You can't be nervous," she said. "I mean, you've done this before."

"Never with a woman I loved," he said, his voice husky with emotion. "Never with a woman who hadn't been with other men. I don't want to hurt you."

"You won't." She unfastened his jeans, remembering the night in the hotel room in Jackson Hole when she had lain awake wondering if he wore boxers or briefs. She smiled when a quick glance showed he was wearing a pair of black briefs with a considerable bulge.

She shivered with anticipation as he unhooked her bra and tossed it on a chair, then eased her panties down her legs.

"A true redhead," he murmured as he tossed her panties on top of her bra, and then he swung her into his arms and carried her to the bed. Holding her against his chest, he drew back the covers, then lowered her to the mattress. He followed her down without ever letting her go, his big body covering hers as he rained kisses over her face and neck and breasts.

Callie moaned softly, every nerve and cell in her body yearning toward him. Her hands moved over him, hungry and restless, loving the feel of his hard-muscled body, the sensual heat of his skin against hers, the taste of his lips.

She wasn't sure when he removed his briefs but she welcomed the feel of him and when he rose above her, his dark eyes filled with love and desire, she was more than ready to receive him. There was a faint moment of discomfort that was immediately forgotten as he began to move within her, worshipping her with his hands and his lips, whispering that he loved her, would always love her.

She quivered with longing, lost in sensations she had never known before, reaching, reaching, for something that eluded her.

"Don't hold back, Red." Cade's voice whispered in her ear. "Just let yourself go. Come on, darlin', you're almost there."

He moved deep inside her and the world exploded in a glorious blaze of sparkling white lights and shimmering rainbows.

She sobbed his name, caught up in the wonder of it, knew she would be eternally grateful that she had waited for this moment, and this man.

Epilogue

Two years later

Callie sat by the big window in the living room, her five-month-old daughter, Marissa, at her breast, her gaze fixed on Cade, who was putting a new colt through its paces.

The last two years had been the happiest of her entire life. She loved living on the ranch with Cade and Jacob. She loved being a wife and a mother. She glanced down at the infant in her arms, certain that no more beautiful child existed anywhere on the planet. Marissa had her father's coppery skin and thick black hair and her mother's gray eyes and upturned nose.

With a sigh of contentment, Callie glanced at the bookshelf across the room, her gaze lingering on a copy of her latest romance—the one with Cade Kills Thunder on the cover.

It was by far her bestselling book to date. Bookstores had ordered twice as many copies as usual. The book had soared to the top of the *New York Times* list and every other bestseller list in the country. She had received hundreds of letters and e-mails from women who wanted to know who the great-looking guy was on the cover. The book had been voted Best Historical Romance and Best Book of the Year at the last conference, and the cover had been awarded top honors, as well. Cade had received letters and phone calls from every publishing house in the business requesting that he pose for the covers of their top-name authors. Of course, he'd had to refuse, informing them that he had an exclusive contract with Callie's publisher. A couple of men's magazines had also approached him, but he had no interest in modeling for anyone but Callie.

It had indeed been a wonderful two years.

She felt her heart skip a beat when she heard Cade's footsteps on the porch; a moment later, he was striding across the room toward her.

"Hey, how are my two best girls?"

"We're fine." Callie winked at him. "How's our favorite cover model and hunk?"

Cade grimaced. "I still can't believe you talked me into doing that again."

"Must be love," Callie teased.

Heat simmered in his eyes. "Must be. Isn't it time to put little Miss Mari down for a nap?"

"Oh, I don't know," Callie remarked, stifling a grin. "I think she looks perfectly happy right where she is."

Cade looked at his daughter, sleeping contentedly against her mother's breast. "Yes," he said drily. "I'm sure she is."

"But?"

"But right now her daddy needs a little attention."

"Ah. And just what kind of attention did you have in mind?"

Bending down, Cade brushed a kiss across her lips. "As if you didn't know."

Callie heaved a mock sigh of resignation. "Oh, very well, if I must, I must."

"Humor me," he said, nibbling her ear. "I'll try to make it worth your while."

"Will you now?"

He nodded, his lips twitching in an effort to keep from laughing. "Think of it as doing research for your love scenes."

Callie burst out laughing. "Gee, how can I resist a romantic offer like that?"

"I'm hoping you won't." Lifting Callie to her feet, he nuzzled her neck, then lightly stroked his daughter's silken cheek. "She's almost as beautiful as you are."

With a sigh, Callie went up on her tiptoes and kissed her husband, then took him by the hand and led him up the stairs, silently thanking the good Lord that it wasn't only romance novels that ended happily ever after.

* * * * *

HARLEQUIN® flipside

It's all about me!

Coming in July 2004,

Harlequin Flipside heroines tell you exactly what they think...in their own words!

WHEN SIZE MATTERS
by Carly Laine
Harlequin Flipside #19

WHAT PHOEBE WANTS
by Cindi Myers
Harlequin Flipside #20

I promise these first-person tales will speak to you!

**Look for Harlequin Flipside
at your favorite retail outlet.**

SILHOUETTE *Romance*®

Author

Nicole Burnham

presents another royal romance...

FALLING FOR PRINCE FEDERICO

(Silhouette Romance #1732)

Prince Federico diTalora always answered the call of duty...to his sons and to his kingdom. But when beautiful relief worker Pia Renati came to stay at the palace, the only call he could hear was the intense beating of his heart!

Available August 2004 at your favorite retail outlet.

SILHOUETTE *Romance*®

COMING NEXT MONTH

#1730 VIRGINIA'S GETTING HITCHED—
Carolyn Zane
The Brubaker Brides
Pragmatic Dr. Virginia Brubaker believed that compatibility—
not love—formed the basis of a lasting marriage. Ranch hand
Colt Bartlett couldn't resist that challenge, and so set out to
prove to the sassy psychologist that it was good old-fashioned
chemistry (and lots of kissing) that kept a marriage sizzling!

#1731 JUST BETWEEN FRIENDS—Julianna Morris
Spoiled little rich girl Kate Douglas may have been way out
of his league, but she was Dylan O'Rourke's best friend and
he'd do anything for her—even accept her temporary marriage
proposal so that she could inherit her grandmother's house.
But he never counted on Kate wanting the *man* more than the
mansion....

#1732 FALLING FOR PRINCE FEDERICO—
Nicole Burnham
Prince Federico diTalora always answered the call of duty...
to his sons and his kingdom. But when beautiful relief worker
Pia Renati came to stay at the palace, the only call he could
hear was the sudden beating of his heart!

#1733 BE MY BABY—Holly Jacobs
When an adorable baby was practically left on confirmed
bachelor Larry "Mac" Mackenzie's doorstep, his first instinct
was to run as fast as he could. But a little help from the thorny,
but seriously sexy Mia Gallagher might prove to this loner that
he was a family man after all....